A Minister in a Box | Aaron Ben-Shahar

D1310979

Translation from The Hebrew: Guri Arad
Contact: bsaaron28@gmail.com

ISBN 9781792763731

A MINISTER IN A BOX

AARON BEN-SHAHAR

PART ONE

CHAPTER 1

Same as every day, Bwana Biko took his morning constitutional, leaving his house on No. 14 Walton St. and walking all the way to the end, at which point he planned to return via the next street. His walk was always the same: he relished looking at the gates of the lavish mansions, often telling his secretary, Edie, his most trusted confidant in London, that the gates of a house are the gateway to one's soul, offering a great deal of insight about the persons residing there, as well as what they do.

Biko referred to No. 16, the house adjacent to his own, as "Tea House". It had three levels, resembled a pagoda of sorts and was a combination of stone and lumber. The front of the house featured a small stone fence with two gates, one for vehicles and the other for persons entering on foot. Both gates were painted green and had copper panels shaped like tea leaves.

He called house No. 18 "Rose House". A hedge with two wooden gates lay between the house and the street. The house itself was relatively modest compared with the others. It spans the width of its grounds, with the front boasting a particularly lovely rose garden.

No. 20 was "Fortress House", complete with a gray wall a little over eight feet tall and an electric iron gate. On rare occasions, Biko spotted a black Bentley driven by a chauffeur leaving the house. The car's dark windows completely obscured its interior.

That morning, as he was walking along, Biko noticed a different car next to Fortress House: a gray van moving very slowly. Before he could get a chance to take one more step, the van beat him to it and stopped right in front of him. The back door opened and two burly men in masks leaped out. Before he knew it, Biko's hands were cuffed behind his back, his mouth was gagged and his eyes were covered by this dark piece of cloth. He tried to cry out through his gag, but the strangers quickly lifted him up and threw him inside the back of the van, face down.

Biko tried to protest, but then he felt a sharp instrument cutting into one of his coat sleeves.

A sharp stab cut through his bare flesh.

Everything around him went dark.

CHAPTER 2

That was to be the happiest day in Bwana Biko's life, but he realized it only at the end of that day.

When he was a second grade student, the teacher always called him "Bwana Biko", but all his fellow students called him "Biko". His mother had told him his father too used to call him by his nickname, "Biko". His father had died when he was two. Biko had no memory of him, except for some dim recollection. In his village, death was not an issue. People were born, they lived and then they died. Their entire lives centered on their struggle to subsist. Having to survive kept them from thinking about their own deaths.

Biko's mother too had very little time to grieve for her husband. At daybreak, the very next day after she buried him, she reported for duty at the corn field, where she picked the cobs clean and gathered them into these large burlap sacks. The fifty naira she was paid for each working day allowed her to buy some flour, sunflower oil and a few other basic groceries to sustain her family.

That day, perhaps later that evening, Biko had planned to play soccer with Osho, his best friend, in a field the village kids used as a playground. As Osho was already running late, Biko went over to his friend's family cabin. Biko was already feeling a sense of foreboding on his way over, having seen Anona, the wailing woman, making her way towards the same cabin he was heading for. That mud hut was no different than any other Biko had been to. It was made of mud bricks complete with straw mats woven from the reed that flourished in the nearby lake. Outside the low, makeshift doorway stood a large clay pot for storing rainwater. The center of the hut's roof had a small hole for letting out the smoke.

The center of the hut's floor usually sported a cooking area, but when Biko arrived, he saw that it was moved to make room for the body of Oubinna, Osho's father. Two palm oil lamps were burning right over the body. Biko could see the mourners by the light they emitted.

Oubinna's two widows lay on either side of his body, wailing and weeping. The first was Osho's mother and the other was Oubinna's first wife, who resided at a nearby hut along with her own children. The family hut was packed full the late Oubinna's numerous children, along with a few of the neighbors, among whom Biko spotted his own mother, who had stopped to pay her respects to the mourners on her way back from the corn field after work.

Upon raising his head to look at the late Oubinna, two things caught Biko's attention: the death mask that was placed over the dead man's face, on which was conferred a sense of peace and resignation. The other was the dead man's bare feet.

Biko was very envious of Osho and his father, as were all the village children, for having their own pair of shoes. Made of deerskin, their shoes sported leather straps they used to firmly fasten the shoes to their ankles. Every now and then, Biko had fashioned himself soles out of palm leaves so as to protect his feet from the dry, burning ground, as well as the jungle thorns, but he knew all too well this hardly came close to constituting proper shoes. On one of his visits to the market at the county town of Benioni, Biko snuck into the cobbler's shop, pointed to a pair of shoes akin to the ones Osho was wearing and asked how much they were.

- One thousand naira.

The cobbler replied dismissively, convinced he wasn't going to make a sale.

'*A thousand naira...*' Biko thought to himself as he was leaving the shoe maker's shop. '*That would be enough for a whole year's supply of yams for the entire family*'. He walked on frustrated and jealous.

There was a time when Osho and his father did not have any shoes. They used to walk barefoot just like everyone else, at least everyone Biko knew. One day, the person Oubinna was working for fell ill, so Oubinna took it upon himself to have Anona, the wailing woman, come sooner than scheduled and honor his employer at his sickbed. He meant it as a parting gesture. The patient was very moved by the visit of the wailing woman, and in this air of grief and illness, took an oath, pledging that should he survive and get better, he would make Oubinna a present of his small plot of palm trees by the lake, which he used to produce oil. Neither the oath taker nor his grateful employee believed he would actually have to live up to his promise, but a miracle nevertheless occurred, and Oubinna's employer did make a complete recovery.

Oubinna and his household were Muslim, whereas his employer was a devout Christian, so when the miracle did transpire, and Oubinna was awarded the plantation as promised, he did not know to whom to give thanks, Jesus or the Prophet Muhammad, or indeed to any of the hoodoo idols so many of the villagers worshiped.

Oubinna stayed on and continued working, doing his manual labor of old at the palm plantation. During the season, when it was time to pick the fruit at his own plot, he picked up a large machete to cut the produce with. He would take Osho and Biko with him to assist in gathering the palms and collecting them into large sacks. He used the palm to make oil, which he then sold to his neighbors. When the crops turned well, he would even have enough to sell at the Benioni market. After a few good seasons, Oubinna had managed to amass enough cash to take Osho with him, where he handed the cobbler a whole two thousand naira as payment for two pairs of shoes, one for himself and one for his son.

Biko was gazing in amazement at the late Oubinna's bare feet when he felt this tug on his arm, pulling him out of the hut. Standing by the huge water jug was Osho. He handed Biko a pair of shoes.

- Here, these are yours. A present from my dad.

Biko was moved to tears. '*Dreams do come true!*' For him, shoes were not merely a means of protection from the street or the forest; they were all he had ever dreamed of ever since he came to his senses. Shoes stood for the transition from poverty, hardship, disheveled schoolbooks, open sewers and monotonous food, to another world, of which he had learned from the old newspapers that he occasionally found at the Sunday market, from stories by passers-by and from his teachers, who told him, much to his astonishment, about places referred to as "libraries", frequented by people wearing shoes, who select any book they wish to read.

Back at Biko's family cabin, a book was never to be seen. This was the same in all the other village huts, as well as the surrounding villages. The only books Biko had ever seen were the tattered schoolbooks available at his school, having already been used by several students before him. You were not allowed to take them off the school premises, so they were kept in a special cabinet at the teachers' lounge.

Biko was studious and hard working. His teachers always said he would go far. Once, they even called his mother to the school and told her, "You have a really gifted son there. You need to let him go to the big city, where he can further apply himself and study more."

Biko's mother was proud of her son, but she did not have the first clue how to move to the big city. Besides, she was at a loss as to where she might find the money to send Biko there.

*

The day after he received his first ever pair of shoes, Biko was absentminded. He waited for school to be over for the day so he could rush over to Mumadi and show him his new pair of shoes. Mumadi was the person Biko admired the most. A sculptor, a wood statue maker, Mumadi lived in a mud hut just like any other villager, yet what set him apart was his sculpting, which was his entire world. He never let go of his chisel, always carving the most striking and outstanding busts. Biko believed that these figures would open their mouths at any time and speak as though they were human. Mumadi also sculpted forest and jungle animals, which Biko often feared could simply wake up, pounce and devour him, or, at the very least, run away back into the jungle.

Every day after school was out, Biko would hurry himself to Mumadi's hut and marvel, excited, at the man's work. Every few weeks, Mumadi would take Biko along with him to the nearby forest, where they would pick a tree for Mumadi's next project. Mumadi preferred to work with ebony, a tree famous for its outer dark bark and white flesh. The villagers referred to ebony as "the baboons' tree" for these monkeys loved to hang from its top branches.

One day, while Mumadi was sitting and carving with Biko watching, a baboon joined them, sitting beside Biko, also looking inquisitively, albeit sadly, at the sculptor's work. Neither Biko nor Mumadi could tell whether the monkey was sad over the ebony that had been taken from him and his congress, or whether he too followed the sculptor's handywork with admiration.

Once a month, Mumadi would pack two large burlap sacks and take the matatu all the way to the market day at the county's main town. The matatu is an old, rundown minibus that circled the nearby lake twice a day. Its route spans through the villages around the lake over this circular dirt road, so the matatu has been the villagers' lifeline. Its busiest day was Sunday, the great market day at the county town of Benioni, so named after the lake. Market day attracted thousands of villagers who all flocked to sell their wares and purchase essential supplies. The market day also attracted many visitors who came from far and wide to soak in the atmosphere. Most of the villagers had arrived on foot the day before, carrying their hard-won crops and picked fruits, for the bus fare, no less than two hundred naira in each direction, was beyond their means. Biko's mother would spend that much on a weekly supply of maize flour. Mumadi, however, could not carry his heavy statues on his back and make the journey on foot. He had to take the matatu. When he took Biko with him, he would pay for his fare as well.

Each day, Biko went to school barefoot, walking about ninety minutes in each direction as he watched the matatu passing him by. For Biko, taking the minibus along with Mumadi was a source of pride and a real experience. He hadn't realized how essential he was to Mumadi: apart from his assistance in carrying the statues and placing them on the wooden stalls, Biko was a natural salesman. He always knew how to captivate the visitors who gathered to watch the ebony figures, spot potential buyers and sell them the artist's works.

Apart from covering his matatu fare, Mumadi paid Biko no wages, except when he made good sales, in which case he would hand the boy two hundred naira, which Biko would then give his mother immediately upon their return to their village.

*

It was about noon at one of those Sunday markets, when a very well-dressed man sporting fine leather shoes stood near Mumadi's stall. He wore a white shirt and black pants, held tightly by a belt made of genuine alligator skin. The man was just standing there in silence for a few moments, until he finally instructed Biko to pack up five statues, for which he paid Mumadi the full asking price without even attempting to haggle. He then loaded them very carefully into an elegant car parked nearby and drove off.

Thrilled, Mumadi and Biko decided the occasion merits a feast in celebration, so they gathered the remaining statues and went over to the nearby stall to have jollof, a yam and goat stew rich in coconut oil, to their hearts' content, along with some rice tea. That was Biko's first taste of this dish, which he always imagined as "rich people's food". He relished the taste for many days after that.

After their meal, Mumadi and Biko took the matatu back to their village, whereupon Mumadi produced the bundle of notes he had received from the mysterious buyer and handed Biko one thousand naira. Biko never held so much money in his entire life. He thanked Mumadi and ran to his family hut, where, in a place known only to himself, he hid two hundred naira. When his mother returned from work, he handed her the remaining eight hundred. This was Biko's very first step to immense fortune.

Next market day, the mysterious buyer appeared yet again as Biko and Mumadi were standing by their stall. He turned to Mumadi:

- I really like your statues. I have this proposition for you: come to Golasa, the capital city, to work for me there. I will find you a place to live and house your statues, for which I shall pay you handsomely. I know this offer is something of a surprise. Think about it. I expect your answer come next market day.

On their next meeting, Mumadi told this mysterious person this:

- I accept your offer, but only on two terms. First, you will be in charge of providing me with the ebony I require. Second, Biko is to come with me.

- I accept both your terms, but this requires both his parents' consent. Let's drive to meet them.

On their way to the car, Biko explained his father could no longer give his consent, so it was really only up to his mother. At the edge of the market, the man invited Biko into the most beautiful car he had ever seen. He sat in the plush car's zebra-leather backseat and guided the driver towards the village of mud huts where he dwelled.

On regular days, Biko would run or power-walk the way from the market back to his village, which took about two hours. The journey by car took half an hour by matatu, whereas this magnificent car covered it in barely ten minutes. '*Oh, the world is certainly full of mystery,*' he thought to himself.

Biko saw his mother doing the washing by the hut. She in turn was astonished to see her son and Mumadi coming out of a fancy car the likes of which she had never seen. Biko went silent, fearful of her reaction to the request the stranger was about to put to her.

- Mom, my name is Buani Robni. I am a merchant from Golasa. I offered Mumadi and Biko to move in with me to the big city. I have gotten to know Biko, and I find him a highly capable boy. I assure you I will take care of him, send him to a good school and see to his every need.

- Since my daughter also moved there four years ago, I have only seen her once.

- I promise you will see Biko at least once a year. Besides, I shall also reimburse you handsomely for the help he would have given you here.

Biko's mother loved him dearly. Besides, in her heart of hearts, she knew her son needed that big break in life.

Packing up Biko's stuff was quick: his entire belongings went into one small burlap bag. Mumadi's possessions did not amount to much either, consisting primarily of his tools, which were secured in the trunk of Buani's car. Before leaving his village, Biko insisted they stop by Osho's hut, where the two friends parted in a tearful embrace.

Biko pointed at his shoes and said, "It's all thanks to them".

As they left the village, they spotted the baboon watching them on the edge of the large forest with such a sad look in his eyes.

*

Biko had never been to the capital before, or to any other city, for that matter. The only city he had ever visited was Benioni, the flat, derelict, county town. Golasa was a shocking marvel on arrival. Having never seen a two-story house before, Biko stared at the tall buildings in amazement, all the more so as they grew even taller the further the car approached the center of town. The plazas, the multitudes in the streets, the traffic jams, the commercial signs, the endless stream of stands and everything else in sight were a source of constant bewilderment for him.

Buani himself negotiated the rush-hour traffic without so much as a sound, completely immersed in his thoughts, apparently unaware of his passengers, until he finally said, "here we are".

These were the very first words Buani uttered since they left Biko's village. The car stopped before a blue barrier, next to which stood a uniformed guard in white, save for a wide brim black hat. The guard saluted, and off the car went, sliding once again along a paved road running through a row of coconut trees, through which Biko could see carefully manicured lawns. The smell of freshly cut grass attested to a recent visit by a gardener. The boulevard culminated at this great mansion, taken right out of Biko's own imagination of stately, heavenly palaces. The manor house was painted white, featuring red tiles and a row of marble columns in the front. The car turned right and drove a while longer before stopping next to small elongated green house.

- This is where you get off. They'll see to you in no time.

Speechless with excitement, both passengers unloaded their few belongings and remained standing on the pavement as the car swerved back towards the palace.

- I am Elizabeth. I am here to look after you two. Come this way.

She had a white, creaseless dress and a white headband. Elizabeth led Mumadi and Biko into the house and showed each of them his assigned room, after which she took Mumadi to an attached spacious building, explaining that per the master's instructions, the annex was to be his study.

- You shall have your supper in the servants' wing, at the back of the manor. The master wishes to meet you both tomorrow at ten in the morning. I will come and take you to him.

Sporting a wide, pearly white smile, Elizabeth left them and went about her business.

Biko was dumbfounded to discover a bed complete with a mattress in his room, in addition to a towel, running water and his own bathroom, all of which were amazing innovations he could not get enough of even in his dreams.

The following morning, Mumadi and Biko, both tired-looking and out of breath, followed Elizabeth, who was all smiles. She led them to Buani's office. He looked at them and said:

- I hope you're being well taken care of. Trunks of ebony will be arriving this very day, along with new tools for you, Mumadi, which I am sure you'll be able to use to turn out fabulous statues like only you can.

Buani then turned to Biko:

- As for you, Biko, as I promised your mother, I shall take good care of you. I sure hope I know what I'm doing. Starting Monday, you will attend the American School, where I hope the teachers will have nothing but good things to tell me about you. And now, if you will both excuse me, I have other matters to attend to.

*

Mumadi did continue to produce the most beautiful statues. He indeed missed the baboons and the scent of the nearby forest, but they were an indelible part of his soul anyway. The spacious studio he was granted, along with the constant supply of ebony and the never ending thrill of this new world he was discovering did him and his work nothing but good. His statues got even better, garnering ever increasing demand.

Mumadi soon discovered that Buani was one of the world's largest African Art merchants, and that he displayed Mumadi's works to the best of his considerable ability, complete with selling them worldwide.

Buani's instincts concerning Biko also proved correct. After a brief period of adjustment, Biko had become the top student in his class. The American School was where the locals attended class along with the children of the elite as well as numerous foreign nationals, the children of the diplomats on assignment to Jeronti, whose capital was home to many internationals. All the students had but one thing in common: their parents could afford the steep tuition fee. Biko excelled not only in his studies, but also in his ability to forge close social ties with is fellow students, displaying striking leadership skills.

Buani took a great interest in Biko and in the development

of the youth's aptitudes. His visits to the school and conferences with the headmaster and the teachers always filled his heart with such content. Having no children of his own, never having married, in fact, Buani's world amounted to the art business, on top of which he had his fingers in lots of other pies, namely oil and real-estate.

After he graduated with honors, Biko went off to study at the London School of Economics. Upon earning his degree, he returned to Jeronti and did very well as a businessman in his own right, gaining a local reputation and a prominent position in the country's top social circles.

*

Ten years passed since Biko had first made Buani's acquaintance. This time, Mumadi wasn't present during their encounter. He was busy ahead of opening his great exhibition in London.

- I scheduled this meeting with you today of all days especially. As you know, it has been ten years to the day since you first arrived here, at my home. I did a great deal to provide you with education and train you to become an outstanding adult. As you may have already learned, succeeding in business requires three things: talent, luck and a knack for working together with the right people. I had a bit of fortune, along with some talent, and as you can tell, my business turned out well. I think that I chose the right people over the years, consistently. My business has been stable in recent years, but of late, perhaps due to my advanced years or simply due to my fatigue, I reached a decision: to focus increasingly on the art world and dedicate most of my time to this pursuit. Knowing you, who possesses such talents, and being so trustworthy, faithful and honest, I would like you to run my business for me.

*

Managing Buani's business opened up a new world for Biko. In addition to his exposure to the local and international business world, for all its many twists and ploys, he eased naturally into a prominent position within Golasa's social elite.

Once a month, Buani would hold a soiree that attracted the very top social and political figures, along with foreign diplomats and dignitaries, who exchanged gossip and insight concerning the world of finance, politics and so on while noshing on the most delectable tidbits and topping up their exquisite drinks, served up by waiters in full livery. Biko was a natural at such events, as though to the manor born, furthering his network of ever deepening ties with the very top people in government, commerce and the arts, both foreign and domestic.

Coupled with his rapid immersion with the cream of Golasa's who's who, Biko also had the good sense to discern on which side his bread was buttered, and how to make sure the layer on his side would always get thicker. One morning, one of the country's largest importers, whom Biko knew from Buani's regular evenings, turned up in Buani's office. At the end of their meeting, the guest produced a large brown envelope from his suit pocket and proceeded to lay a few piles of notes bound in rubber bands on Biko's desk, and off he went.

- I need your help, Biko. I need to run along to a meeting. Please deposit these funds in my bank account."

Biko arrived at the bank accompanied by one of his security men, where, much to his surprise, he was given a receipt for one hundred thousand naira. This was hardly the first bundle of cash to exchange hands at Buani's home or office, where many an oil magnet came by, along with major importers, coconut oil merchants and other assorted businessmen, each of whom never failed to leave behind a stuffed brown envelope.

*

It was during one of those parties at Buani's mansion that Biko, customarily mingling, glass of champagne in hand, busy fostering new ties and tending to existing contacts, gasped. All the way at the other end of Buani's great hall, he saw this butterfly of a woman hovering ever so gracefully from one guest to another. It was none other than Bashira, his sister. That very split second, she recognized her own brother as well. They each made their way through the crowd in the other's direction, until they finally fell into one another's arms, asking simultaneously, "What are you doing here?"

Before they could get a chance to retire to a remote and discrete corner, their behavior astounded everyone, for the sight of two attractive young people kissing and embracing in public was hardly an everyday occurrence. Bashira took her brother by the hand and led him to one of the guests, a fellow sporting very elegant attire.

- May I present my husband, Shagray. This is Biko, my brother.

One could hear Shagray's sigh of relief all the way to the other side of the hall. Biko pulled Buani towards him.

- May I present Bashira, my sister. My mother told you about her.

Having satisfied the curiosity of some of Buani's guests,

setting the minds of some of them at ease, Biko and Bashira finally found a peaceful corner to speak.

Bashira was the most beautiful girl in their village, with so many friends and beaus. Aged fourteen, having consulted with her mother, she decided to accept a job offer, to serve as a maid at one of Golasa's richest households. Moving to the capital did her nothing but good, but the distance caused her ties with her family back at the village to fray. Biko was merely a small boy when she left, so he had grown up missing her all those years, inducing him to promise his mother as well as to himself that he would look for Bashira. And lo and behold, here she is - at Buani's manor! The two spoke at length, trying to catch up as best they could and make up for all those lost years and mutual longings. When the party wound down, Shagray joined them.

- Here he is, my wonderful husband and father to my two kids. I am watching the both of you and can already tell what firm friends you two are going to be.

And indeed so it was. The friendship between Shagray and Biko grew stronger and they became close friends. Already one of the leaders of Jeronti's ruling party, Shagray soon became party leader. In the meantime, Biko's business thrived. Then, in the framework of an atypical development in its history, Jeronti held democratic elections, culminating in Shagray's election as president. Soon after assuming office, he called Biko.

- Thank you for your kind wishes, but it takes more than mere well wishing to build a country. I require your assistance. We've got major problems. On the one hand, we have this underground movement getting stronger up in the north, and on the other, we're faced with grave economic problems. I need to put together a government consisting of people I can trust implicitly, and you're one of them.

- What would you have me do?

- Serve as minister for transport and minerals, including the oil business. You of all people know how important the energy sector is to this country.

After much deliberation, and having consulted Buani at length, Biko informed Shagray he was ready to assume his role as minister.

*

Biko was a quick study, rapidly learning the ropes and realizing the enormous power his new position afforded him. He was focused on promoting the country's infrastructure, but his primary duties lay with the oil industry, seeing as Jeronti lived and breathed oil, its ultimate export commodity. Most of the country's wealthy people were connected with the energy sector. You could not drill for oil, export it or construct any storage facilities without a government permit, which was exclusively Biko's purview.

One day, the manager of an Italian oil drilling company showed up at his office, a short while after receiving a license to drill offshore. After exchanging a few pleasantries, his guest asked, "Where shall I transfer your commission?"

Biko was aghast, but he hid it well.

- I will get back to you soon.

Then, he rushed over to meet with Buani and tell him about the manager's offer.

- I thought you were in the loop.

Buani laughed and continued.

- What did you think? Where do you think all these great big houses, fancy cars and living it up come from?

- What commission was he talking about? And how do you receive it? Do you suppose he'll coming bearing a brown envelope?

- Don't worry, there are clear rules about these things. The Italian knows precisely how much he should pay. I can now see you're completely clueless about these matters, so let me tell you this: large sums are involved, and not in naira, mind you.

- Where should he transfer the money to? My bank account here only has a few thousand naira after my paycheck is drawn.

- No one keeps their funds here in Jeronti. First of all, it's best to keep this sort of thing under wraps. Secondly, there could be a coup anytime, and the first thing the new government would do is throw you in jail and take all your money.

- So what am I to do?

- Go to London.

- And then what?

- You'll go and see a solicitor, John Henry Byrot, Esq., a dear man. Tell him I sent you, and he'll tell you what to do. But be quick about it. The Italians have a short memory.

*

It was at Byrot's chambers on Bailey St. soon thereafter that Biko's eyes had opened. During their meeting, which lasted for several hours, he learned of existing secret accounts, front organizations and all sorts of trusteeships, not to mention the involvement of his newly found solicitor in all this.

The very next day, upon Biko's return to Jeronti, he saw the Italian manager at his office and read out to him, using a small note he kept in his pocket, the details of his secure account in

Panama City. Once the Italian had gone, Biko destroyed the note per Byrot's instructions, flushing the remains down the toilet. A few days later, he received a call from the London solicitor, who intimated to him, using specific code words, that a sum of one million dollars was deposited in Biko's Panama City bank account.

Biko soon got the hang of it, realizing very early on he need not even ask for any commission: the bribes simply fell into his lap on a regular basis from those seeking his favors. He himself made a point of visiting London often, with every opportunity used to receive further instructions and clarifications concerning the destination of his funds, be it the Cayman Islands, the Channel Islands and numerous other hideouts - in addition to Panama City.

Biko also kept close and constant contact with his sister. Once a year, they would send a car round to fetch their mother from the remote village. As much as their aged mother was happy to see her children and throw her arms around her grand kids, she nevertheless could hardly wait for her return to her mud hut. Having slept her entire life on a straw mat and used to cooking over an open fire, she could never get used to the luxury and comfort her two children bestowed on her. She did acquiesce to one thing, though, and even that took a great deal of persuasion: to retire from her hard labor at the corn fields, where she had been working since she turned fourteen. She agreed to receive a small annuity from her children, which sufficed her to get by and spend her days gossiping with her old time village friends.

*

The jungle was all aflutter, complete with the sound of drums and battle cries rising from the forests and mud huts. The militia was counting the days before the order was given. This was no longer a fledgling guerilla of malcontents, but rather an organized army, fully equipped and disciplined, as its commanders knew how to use the resources under their domain to establish highly skilled formations over time, until they were ready for action.

Instability set in at Golasa and the other major cities. Major demonstrations and strikes had now become the norm, and the general atmosphere was one of shaky ground, fueled by Jeronti's economic hardships. The people were starving, so they got together, ready to take action.

*

Biko was very close to his brother in law, the president. They used to meet every now and then and discuss their country's problems - in particular the threat to the government, primarily posed by militia commander Mkume Imru, who was gaining notoriety for his cruelty as well as valor.

During their last meeting, Shagray said to Biko:

- I am glad you've come to me. My intelligence bureau is reporting Imru intends to mount an assault on Golasa. I do not believe my army will be capable of standing up to the militia, and I know what's waiting for me, my family, you and the rest of my friends, once they take the capital. I decided to send my wife and kids to London this very day. I myself am leaving by private jet thanks to a last minute favor I called in. I suggest you do the same. Better have an escape plan in place. In any case, I made sure you would get a head's up forty-eight hours in advance so that you may have enough time to get organized and leave Jeronti.

Biko rushed over to part from his sister, who was waiting for him at her own home, where she greeted him with dozens of suitcases already packed. They resolved to meet again the first chance they would get. Two days later, Biko received an urgent messenger from his brother in law, writing to tell him: "It's time."

Biko took a small suitcase he had prepared in advance, got into his own car and drove towards the border with Benin, the neighboring country. At a gas station close to the border, he walked into the restroom, where he changed into a priest's habit, typical of the many Christian denominations there. Biko's numerous precautions seemed superfluous. The border guard didn't even bother to look at him when he stamped Biko's passport at the small, sleepy post. Biko then proceeded to drive to Porto Novo, the capital of Benin, where he boarded a regular KLM flight to, then took another flight to London. Upon his arrival at Heathrow, he called a cab to Bailey St., which took him straight into the open arms of his solicitor, John Henry Byrot, Esq.

*

Shortly after Biko's arrival in London, he was called to a meeting with the head of Scotland Yard, at the aid of Attorney Byrot, during which he told his story and asked for political asylum on the grounds the new government of Jeronti might be hot on his tail. Biko also raised his concerns that criminal elements might be after his money. Attorney Byrot lent further credence to his client's motion, noting the substantial contribution to the UK's economy a man in Biko's position can make. The chief of Scotland Yard agreed to look into Biko's request for asylum, noting it still had to go by proper channels through the Ministry of Immigration. After consulting with the Home Office and the Foreign Office, it was decided to grant Biko a temporary immigration status, valid for a three-year period. Upon the official granting, Biko was made clear the UK was not to be held accountable for his personal safety - apart from its general responsibility to keep the peace. He was further advised that the police do not possess the financial resources to provide close security, so in case he was concerned for his safety, he had better hire a private security detail. That said, Scotland Yard's intelligence branch did keep a file on him, including Biko on its list of persons featuring a high security risk.

*

Biko chose Kensington as his permanent lodgings. The house he found afforded him both the creature comforts and personal safety he felt he required. A two-story house, rather remote and detached from his neighbors' houses. The first floor consisted of a spacious guestroom, a kitchen and bathroom, in addition to a separate wing that housed Biko's study and an adjacent room for Edie, his secretary. The office had its own back exit. The second floor featured bedrooms with adjoining bathrooms.

During the first three months of living there, and per the advice of the police, Biko did avail himself of a private security firm, whose car parked up front the entire time, complete with its men carrying out regular rounds and patrols. But then, Biko put a stop to this, for one thing due to his neighbors' complaints of the disturbance all this constituted, as well as his sense of security and safety having been restored as the months went by. Once he dismissed his security details on short announcement, Biko did install panic buttons throughout the house.

Each morning, Biko would await Edie's arrival. Once she came in for work at their office, he would take his stroll up and down the quiet street. After his morning constitutional and morning coffee, he would go into his study, go over the mail, look into his finances and read the papers, paying careful attention to any news of his homeland. Biko kept abreast of all developments back in Jeronti, maintaining close contact with those among his friends who were still living there. He followed events closely in the hope of better days to come.

Edie was a highly dominant figure in Biko's life. She was his friend, confidant, and right arm in all matters. She genuinely liked him and appreciated him. Concerned for his safety and devoted to him, her care for him knew no end. Every morning, when he went out the door, she followed his receding figure until he turned behind the corner. She regained her composure only when he was back safely in the house. This was her regular custom each morning, until her worst fears came true.

CHAPTER 3

"*Allahu Akbar!*"

The cry sent shivers of shock down the back of every member of the militia as they stood at attention, causing them to freeze, despite being strong in numbers, complete with hundreds of men and boys standing in tight formation. Even the monkeys at the treetops around the clearing went silent. Then, a boy leaped from one of the columns, a drawn sword in his arm, and was about to stab the militia commander, Mkume Imru, with it. A split second later, another boy drew the sword one of the militia officers was carrying and cut the would-be assassin's throat.

There was a great deal of commotion, as the commanders began shouting all sorts of orders no one could make out and boys dispersed, letting out cries of fear. Even the monkeys resumed their screaming.

After things had calmed down a bit, Imru tuned to the boy and asked:

- What's your name?
- Mkume Shibu, sir.
- What tribe do you belong to?
- Ibu, sir.
- How did you get here?

- The chieftain decreed that each family would put one child up for the militia, so my mother decided I would be the one to come over to you.

'The Heroes Militia' acquired a reputation of being tough and ruthless. Dominating large parts of Jeronti, it soon began collecting 'protection tithes' from the plantation owners: pineapple, coconuts and palms, as well as rice fields and corn plots. In addition, the area under its control was rich in oil, so any company interested in operating in those regions had to pay high protection fees. The militia recruited its soldiers from among the many volunteers who flocked to its ranks, be it on ideological grounds or in the hope of eking out a living. The militia filled its quotas of men by levying families, forcing them to recruit at least one boy per family, one of whom was Mkume Shibu.

- I like the boy. I shall appoint him as my personal aid.

And so it was that they came to meet one another, a fourteen year old Ibu boy named Shibu and Mkume Imru, the highly admired commander of 'the Heroes Militia'.

*

Shibu was a clever youth, full of energy and creativity. He was also fiercely loyal to his commander. Over time, he gained Imru's confidence to such an extent, he had become his confidant.

One day, Shibu was summoned to Imru's cabin, which consisted of mud bricks just like the other ones. From the outside, it was different from them only in terms of its size. It sported stylish mats, complete with fabulous cushions, presented to Imru by the various chieftains. In addition to the customary ceiling vent, the cabin also had several windows that let in more light, a welcome feature augmenting the traditional co-conut-oil lit lamps. The center of Imru's cabin lacked the typical pyre used for heating and cooking. Rather, it had a huge bowl filled with all sorts of fruit. Shibu had long since taken note of his commander's penchant for fruit, so he made sure he was always kept in excess of fresh, fragrant produce. Imru had on his usual white robe with golden threads. He was always barefoot, too. Another constant feature was his red beret, which he swore he'd replace for the traditional headdress once secure at the presidential palace in Jeronti's capital city. When Shibu entered Imru's cabin, he saw him seated on one of his cushions. In a rare gesture, Imru began peeling a large mango, which he then proceeded to divide between the two of them. "I appoint you commander of the forces fighting the government's army," Imru told Shibu.

The militia was growing stronger all the time, and its dominion over large areas began posing a threat to Jeronti's central government, which did send its forces to subdue the rebels every now and then. Nevertheless, the opposition was highly motivated, to the point of dealing the regular army a series of blows culminating in their shameful retreat time and again.

- Thank you, sir. I shall not let you down. To victory!

One day, an officer from the rank and file of the militia's field command walked into Imru's cabin in the middle of a staff meetings.

- We've caught the government army's chief, a general. We are going to kill him.

- Hang on. Bring him to me!

The defeated chief was brought in before Imru, all bruised and beaten black and blue. His hands and feet were bound. He knew the score all too well.

- Untie him!

Imru then said, "Give him some water," much to everyone's surprise.

- What's your name?

- Nburu Shimu, General.

- Let me make you a once in a lifetime offer: I'll cut you loose, your soldiers too, those who are still alive. You'll all go back to Golasa and say you've won the battle and killed many of our people.

Nburu, who had already reconciled himself to his fate, looked in disbelief at the militia commander, who was infamously ruthless.

- But... what is it that you want of me?

- Nothing at all. Just bear in mind who it was who gave you your life back. Every so often, keep my men posted as to the developments at Golasa.

Right before General Nburu left, Imru gave him a large sum of money and furnished his men with old arms and military equipment, "spoils of war", as it were, to be used as 'photo ops' for their alleged victory over the militia upon returning to Golasa. This way, the militia established its own powerbase of collaborators within the government, in anticipation of the right time to launch a successful coup.

*

Shibu was summoned to Imru's cabin once again. This was right after yet another victory in a succession of campaigns in the course of which the chieftains 'donated' further protection fees and witnessed the militia's growing power.

- What is it, chief?

- We never got to talk about personal matters or about my own plans. I think it's time.

Imru's face, which also imbued boldness, now struck Shibu with a look of deep thought.

Imru took a sip of palm wine and spoke softly.

- It's time for me to take over the reins of government and bring order back to this country.

- Yes, sir.

- I never told you this, Shibu, but the day you saved my life and told me how you came to join our ranks, you reminded me of myself back when I was your age. I too, much like you, lived miserably in a mud hut, only to be sold off at the age of fourteen by my father, because he could not afford to feed us all. Nevertheless, both of us were saved by having been sold off: you were sent to us, whereas I was sent off to become a servant at one of the richest families in Golasa. They had enormous coconut plantations over at the delta region. Fortunately for me, they were kind and generous. They sent me to learn English. They made sure the help got an education. But I never forgot where I came from. I realized the famine and poverty I found at the capital were no different from where you and I had come from. Some people get to live like royalty, robbing our country blind, letting everyone else live on mere scraps, on one hundred naira a day, barely enough for a daily meal.

Shibu was amazed to see how gloomy his commander's face turned. Had he not learned first-hand of his ferocity, he could have sworn he saw a tear running down the corner of Imru's eye.

- When I was older, I told that generous family I was leaving them, that I wanted to go back to my family. I took a vow to vanquish evil, right wrongs, so I founded the militia. Everyone thinks the militia I created is cruel. Perhaps it is. But I know everything has been for the sake of a greater cause. Yesterday, I returned from a tour of the delta region, where I reached this village in the middle of large coconut plantations. I was taken aback by the sight of dozens of boys, all crippled and severely injured. Turns out that their sole source of livelihood is picking the coconuts. That is something only young boys can perform. More often than not, they fall to their deaths all the way from the treetops - or break their necks or limbs. These stingy plantation owners won't even spare them a ladder. They have to climb up and risk their lives. I was approached by this boy, both whose legs were amputated, as well as his arm. He asked me for a handout. I gave him a hundred naira note. When I saw how his eyes lit up, it hit me that things could not go on like that anymore. We have got to change the way things are going.

Imru proceeded to take another slice of fruit, gesturing the meeting was over.

*

One rainy morning, a special messenger sent by General Nburu appeared at Imru's cabin, reporting about the utter paralysis back at Golasa. The soldiers had not been paid for several months, so they called a strike. Starving people were staging demonstrations everywhere, and looting, robbery and murder were becoming widespread. The general atmosphere at the capital was one of despair on the one hand, and nervous anticipation on the other.

In response, Imru called Shibu and said, "It's time!"

It didn't take the militia long to mount its assault. The order was given, and off the rebel forces went, heading for Golasa, attacking it from several flanks, meeting no serious opposition. They soon assumed control over the entire government, immediately after which Imru called a curfew and instructed his soldiers to shoot anyone on sight if they broke curfew. He also ordered the immediate arrest of all government members and officials, having dozens of them executed without trial. Imru's men proceeded to seize control of the regular army. Any officers with prior ties to Imru were summarily promoted as generals in the revolutionary army, whereas those who opposed the militia were executed forthwith.

Imru also seized control of Jeronti's economy. Adamant on his vision of how the way the country should be run, he was steadfast about ousting most of the chief figures, leaving in place only a few key officials in order to maintain continuity and stability, so as not to undermine the country's foreign trade and international relations.

The very first evening of the militia's takeover of Golasa and the other major cities, along with additional key positions, Imru convened a major meeting at the presidential palace.

- We have won the day! I now proclaim the new Republic of Jeronti!

Imru then gave a speech before the hundreds of his rejoicing men: "I hereby appoint myself as president of the republic. I pledge to serve the people honestly and faithfully. Jeronti will no longer be a corrupt country with crooked leaders. It shall have a government that will work for the good of its citizens!"

He proceeded to make an impassioned gesture before hundreds of cheering officers, taking his red beret off and replacing it with a headdress of white and gold, symbolic of peace, as worn by the elders of the Ibu tribe.

Imru's next move came immediately after the mass meeting. He convened a small council of war, before which he announced the militia was hereby disbanded. He then laid out his plans for the near future and announced Shibu's appointment as his chief of staff, complete with far reaching authorities and powers.

CHAPTER 4

- Do not play with them punks from Dora!

- Don't you worry, mom, I'm only going to the beach with some friends from the village.

Then, he asked his friend as follows when they met up at the beach:

- Say, Dudi, why does my mom refer to you guys as "those punks from Dora"?

- Your mom is right. We have many punks down at the Dora Projects. Inner city, you know. No, you don't know what's it like: whenever we see someone running down the street, we know for sure he's being pursued by someone with a knife.

- Are you a criminal too? When I told my mom I would like you to come to my Bar Mitzvah, she said I mustn't dare invite you, so as not to shame my grandparents.

- No matter. Let's go to the market and poach some oranges, then.

*

Dudi Dayan and Assaf Shlomi were bosom buddies. Their first encounter took place at the beach, where they had hung with their friends each and every day. Dudi, the leader of the gang from Dora, was olive skinned and had bright brown eyes. Assaf was an assertive blond guy from the nearby village. They both had much in common, though, from their height, through their handsome features to their dominant demeanors, which all propelled them to the position of unofficial leadership of their respective packs. They soon realized no girl would come between them and undermine their kinship. One day, Assaf heard a girl named Nili turning to Dudi and saying, "they say you are an expert in French kissing!" to which Dudi replied, "that's not true, I am an expert in Moroccan kissing!"

Everything clicked for Assaf there and then. He himself liked Miri, who was herself from Dora, with her brown skin and pearly white teeth, rather than the company of the girls from his own village, whom he had known since preschool.

Assaf and Dudi would meet every day at the beach, either alone or as part of their larger groups, and flirt with the girls. Then, Dudi would run for fifteen miles along the shore, whereas Assaf preferred to brave the waves and surf.

*

- Where were you this past week? I was looking all over for you.

- I did time.

- What time?

- I was in jail, you moron…

- Oh. What did they put you in jail for?

- They caught me driving a stolen car.

- But why did you steal a car? Didn't you tell me your family used to be rich back in Morocco, that your dad had a brand new Citroën?!

- You just don't get it. You never will. It's got nothin' to do with the car, it's all about the thrill, the excitement, it's about sticking it to the man, breaking the rules, doing whatever you g-dam* well please. When I'm doin' time, I feel like a free man, knowing that it is those jailors who are actually behind bars. I walk into my cell with a smile, and when I come out, I smile even wider.

Assaf brought it up once again a few days later.

- You know, Dudi, I keep thinking about your arrests. What's it like to be in a prison cell?

- That depends on who or what you are, a man or a doormat. For me, an arrest is a kind of experience, an opportunity to meet other people, a new, higher perspective on the law, and test I put myself through.

- And how do you pass the time?

- Oh, time flies! I meet the most fascinating people, from company chiefs to the pettiest criminal, and realize that after all, they could not be more equal, and besides, they all need me, since I am strong and experienced. You can take my word for it, 'doing time' is a far greater experience than those trips you take to Sinai and sleep in shabby tents and the like.

- I'm intrigued.

- So. You'd like to give it a try? I have an idea for you. How about this: I have to report to a cell this Sunday, for five days. Go in my place, why don't you.

- Are you nuts? Me? Under arrest? And why should they put me there instead of you?

- If this is something you wanna experience, you will find out just how easy it would be to trade places with me. You have until Sunday to think about it.

That Sunday, Assaf reported for duty at the prison, right

after telling his parents he was going on holiday to Eilat for a few days. When he produced Dudi's ID, the guard on duty didn't even raise his head to look at him. He simply pushed a button and opened the iron door to let Assaf in. Then, wearing nothing but his briefs, Assaf proceeded to pass a short security check, had his few effects stored and was summarily led to a cell, which he shared with eight other inmates.

Assaf spent the days in his cell talking to the other inmates, who were there on merely a daily basis, so rotation kept things interesting for him. Five days of incarceration later, he heard Dudi's name on the PA system. Next, the guard on duty handed him Dudi's ID back along with the rest of his personal effects, and off he went, free and clear, straight to Dudi's embrace outside the prison.

- Well? How'd it go?

- Not that bad, actually, just like you said. Nevertheless, once was enough.

A few days went by, and Assaf turned to Dudi and said as follows:

- Now it's your turn to replace me.

- What do I have to do?

- I told you I had enrolled in the IDF Junior Command Preparatory School in Haifa. One of the entry exams is a ten-mile run. I don't think I am up for it, so I am asking you to run for me.

- Why would they let me run as you?

- Don't worry, they don't even ask for an ID. There are eight hundred and sixty candidates. Just show up and run at Tirat HaCarmel Beach, sign up in my name, and everything will be all right.

Assaf was waiting for Dudi at the end of the run.

- How did it go?

- Don't worry, you passed your exam. I was actually in first place the whole time, but I didn't wanna stick out too much, so I moved to third place.

*

The two friends continued to meet daily, until the time came for Assaf to go to that army school. After graduation, he joined the Paratroopers Commando. He rushed over to the beach on one of his very first leaves to find Dudi.

- So, Dudi, you're in the Special Forces, too, right? What battalion?

- None. I volunteered, but once they found out who I was, they wouldn't hear of it. They made me do menial gardening and all sorts of other s*itty jobs at this camp nearby. They don't know what kind of combat fighter they've lost.

Assaf went on to officer training course, which he graduated with honors, after which he received his first command. Shortly thereafter, he was promoted to deputy company commander. Three months before his compulsory service was due to end, the brigade commander asked to see him.

- You are on the fast track for command. As soon as you sign up as a career officer, you can have command of your own company. I do believe you're going to be our youngest ever commander, the youngest in the entire history of the Paratroopers Commando.

- Thank you, sir, but I don't think I am going to stay on as a career officer. I am going to uni.

Despite the surprised commander's best attempts, Assaf remained adamant.

As soon as he left the IDF, Assaf registered for a double major in economics and international relations at the Hebrew University in Jerusalem. He saw less and less of Dudi, and they became estranged.

One morning, while hanging out with friends on the uni's lawn, one of his fellow students told him he had heard Dudi was charged with murder and was in prison, awaiting trial.

*

Assaf was so dedicated that he graduated his first major in two academic years. As soon as got his diploma, he sent two identical letters, one to the Ministry of Defense, and the other to the Ministry of Foreign Affairs:

Re: Employment in Your Department

Sir,
I, Assaf Shlomi, hereby apply for a post at the ministry.

I served in a Special Forces unit and have recently earned my BA in International Relations. I am also studying economics and am considering a degree in law as well.

I am confident my abilities would make an ample contribution to the ministry's operations.

I await your soonest reply.

Yours faithfully,

Assaf Shlomi

Three weeks after sending both letters, Assaf received a white envelope without any markings, except for his name and address in handwriting. Inside was a typed reply:

Attn. Assaf Shlomi
Re: Meeting

Dear Sir,
You are hereby invited to a meeting at 14:00, 12 Peretz St., Apt. 3, Tel Aviv.

Assaf showed up at the appointed time. The houses in that area were old, having been built back in the 1930s. The whole environment spoke of dereliction, and the front of the three-story house at No. 12 was no different. It was just as rundown, with the walls coming apart at the seams, exposing rusty iron beams. Over by the entrance, Assaf saw the mailboxes with handwritten names. The spot for apartment three was blank.

As he climbed the first flight of stairs, he noticed that apartment one on the ground floor had a sign for a young couple. The first floor had two doors with the numbers 1 and 2, respectively. Nothing else. He rang the bell at No. 3. The door opened immediately, and he could see colorful floor tiles and high ceiling, so typical of those 1930's buildings. The room on the right was empty. The tiny kitchen, also by the entrance, had no appliances whatsoever, so Assad surmised no one had been living there for quite some time. The other room was also empty, save for a simple wooden desk at the center, with two chairs on either side. The desk had a pitcher of water with two glasses. The elderly man sitting there rose to greet Assaf as he entered the room and shook his hand.

- Kalman's the name. Do sit down.

Assaf was dumbfounded. As a graduate of foreign relations studies, he expected a post as aide to the Israeli Ambassador in Paris, at the very least, or the strategic advisor on international affairs to the minister of defense. The unfolding interview wasn't to his liking.

- Who are you, sir? What is this place?

- We are meeting on account of your letter.

Kalman's face spoke of fatigue and an air of someone who's seen it all before.

- Patience. All will be revealed to you in due course.

'*Very well then, I'll play along,*' Assaf thought to himself. Kalman spent an hour interrogating him primarily concerning general issues, asking very few personal questions. All throughout his inquiries, Kalman was the very picture of boredom and aloofness. At the end, he handed Assaf a four-page questionnaire to fill and mail back to an address he wrote for him on the back of the forms.

Upon returning to his apartment, Assaf realized the forms covered numerous details, including his family, friends and three references. That bit was easy enough: he immediately filled in the name of his high school manager, his regiment commander, and a relative who was in charge of a high security factory.

Another three weeks went by, and another envelope came in, summoning Assaf Shlomi to another meeting. This time, Kalman appeared more alert and engaged, asking more direct questions, this time. He was also raising personal stuff, straight out of the questionnaire forms. Then, he asked Assaf:

- Is there any particular reason you did not mention Dudi Dayan in your list of friends?

The cat nearly got Assaf's tongue. He did consider filling Dudi's name in. For one thing, they drifted apart almost entirely. Besides, adding Dudi's name would garner Assaf no bonus points, to say the least.

- Well, I could have told you there wasn't any room on the form for any more friends' names, and I did complete it in full. But truth be told, I did consider it, but ended up deciding not to include him, because I can't say for sure we are friends anymore.

Assaf realized he misjudged Kalman. '*I must remember no to be taken in by his standoffish and gloomy demeanor, especially seeing as on my last visit home, my mom pulled me away to the shed, where she told me the neighbor, Jochebed, had told her in strictest confidence that some men came by, saying they were from the ministry of defense, and asked all sorts of questions about our family.*'

- I also know you people know Dudi was found guilty of murder and is doing time, but that's not why I omitted his name.

- And what is your opinion of Dudi?

- I think he's quite a guy, a loyal friend. He did goofy stuff. I was sad to hear about his troubles, and I sure hope they'll be over for him soon.

Three weeks later, another white envelope. Kalman was much more pleasant at this new meeting, offering him water and pouring him.

- I am glad to inform you that you have been accepted to work for the Mossad!

Assaf was allowed no time to respond. '*The Mossad of all*

places?! I never sought a position there?!' He was familiar with Israel's covert intelligence service of course. He took part in a several operations behind enemy lines, in Lebanon, and it was rumored some of the members of the force were Mossad. That was back during his military service. *'I never imagined I'd be working for the Mossad!'*

- They'll be calling you up in a few days. Good luck and all the best!

Kalman left no doubt the meeting was over.

Straight after that, Assaf went to Bat Yam, a beach town south of Tel Aviv. Its famed Cliff Beach was his favorite spot for quiet thought, whenever he needed to relax and concentrate. The white sands, yellow cliffs, and blue waters gave him the peace of mind and bold resolution he required. *'Well, if life has led me to the Mossad, let it be. That must be the best thing for me.'*

He got in without a hitch. Having graduated basic Mossad training with honors, he was assigned to the operations department, where he excelled, shining brightly on each mission, however complex. He rose in the ranks very rapidly, securing a position as head section chief very quickly. His planned operations were imaginative as they were bold, resolute, focused and inspired.

*

In addition to his operational duties, Assaf placed himself at the disposal of the training department, making a point of appearing before each new class of recruits. His lectures soon became legendary, a large audience, before whom he outlined the organizational doctrine boiled down as follows:

1.*"For by wise counsel thou shalt make thy war"* (Proverbs 24:6).

"Sophistication, originality, creativity and initiative are the basis for intelligence as a discipline, as a line of work," Assaf explained to his class. He then further elaborated. "One day, one of our operatives in Amman sent information according to which an Islamic Jihad cell was poised to carry out a terrorist attack in Eilat. They were supposed to be driven over to Wadi Rum, spend the night there and reach Eilat on foot in the morning. Two days before their scheduled assault, a herd of sheep made camp at the wadi, along with three shepherds. When the terrorists arrived, one of them went over to check the shepherds out. He was satisfied they were benign, so he went back to his fellow cell members. That very night, those 'shepherds' rose up and eliminated the terrorists, thereby averting a major terrorist attack in Eilat."

He then proceeded to introduce another maxim:

2. *Hesitation shows wisdom - indecisiveness is weakness*

"A terrorist organization in some country in the southern part of Africa was planning to target a Jewish center," Assaf recounted. "They prepared a car bomb and planned to detonate it inside the compound. We uncovered their plan in time and managed to trace the car's hiding place. The next day, our team waited out on the street for the car's drive that morning into the Jewish center. When they closed in, they saw, much to their surprise, the car had two additional passengers on top of those they already knew about: two women. Our team in the field didn't know what to do. After hesitating for quite a bit, they finally decided not to intercept the car. Those two women got off after a few blocks and the car went on into that Jewish organization, where it blew up, causing lots of casualties. That right there is an example of wisely hesitating yet being woefully indecisive, with horrendous repercussions."

Assaf then went on to make further points and elaborated using anecdotes.

3. *Pity is a form of cruelty.*

"Obeying the law and observing human values are at the core of any intelligence operation. Nevertheless, an operative may find him or herself in a difficult spot, at times, and, as fate would have, those crises surface at the least convenient time. When they occur, rise above them, get over any emotions you may have, and stick to the mission at hand."

4. *"When you have to shoot, shoot, don't talk."*

"This unforgettable line by Eli Wallach playing Tuco in *The Good, The Bad and the Ugly*, is chock-full of military insight of the very first order: if you decide on a particular action, do it. Any talk that is devoid of resolution and confidence is a sure sign of weakness, which is in turn a recipe for failure."

5. *"In quietness and in confidence shall be your strength"* (Isaiah 30:15).

"An intelligence campaign must be founded on silence and mystery. Whosoever has joined us for the sake of bolstering their ego had better look for a different job. We do not have fanfare, nor do we stage any grand spectacles. We are governed by silence. This also goes for your spouses as well as for your children. Good intelligence is based on the human element. Nothing new has come on the scene since Joshua sent two men to spy secretly, and they met Rahab of Jericho. The only difference is our use of the term 'agents'. An agent cannot operate in another country without embracing this maxim of 'in quietness'. Now, 'confidence' stands for the main characteristic of an operative: he or she is confident of their goal being righteous. Be confident that should anything happen to you, every friend you've got will do everything they can to save you."

6. *"Flatter as little as possible and do not fear criticism."*

"Compliments often miss their point. Being overly satisfied with yourself makes you less alert and therefore less motivated. Worthy criticism makes you want to be better, try harder and rectify those faults. The Mossad has no room for anyone who cannot take criticism."

7. *"Thorough planning: beforehand; in-depth study: after"*

"These principles are the prerequisite for any successful operation. Proper, methodical planning ahead of any action constitutes about sixty percent of the entire mission. Investigating the operation as exhaustively as possible after it's done prevents sixty percent of the problems in the next mission."

*

Assaf Shlomi's brilliant career in Operations was marred by only one affair. Generally referred to as "the Isfahan affair", few have actually heard about it. The committee assigned to investigate what had happened consisted of the Mossad's chief himself, his deputy and the legal counselor, who wrote up the meetings' protocol by hand. When the committee concluded, they summoned Assaf to update him on their conclusions.

- As you know, we spent days and nights on investigating this affair, and ultimately found you were not personally to blame for the failure. We examined the operation as a whole, went over each element and studied the intelligence at your disposal prior to the mission, along with the logistic infrastructure. We also realized what the objective difficulties that you've encountered were. So much for your personal responsibility. That said, we cannot ignore the fact that we lost three of our best agents. In addition, we lost a major source and our deterrence was undermined. Consequently, although you were not personally accountable, we nevertheless decided you shall no longer be involved in operational activity.

- May I be allowed to say my piece?

- You have that right, but you did say everything you had to say before the committee. Case closed.

After the committee dispersed, the Mossad's chief asked Assaf to remain there.

- I know how difficult that decision was for you, but you also know we had no choice. Nevertheless, we do not want to lose you. I consulted with my colleagues and can offer you to head our international division. It's a new department we are about to establish. You may have forty-eight hours to mull it over and return here, to my office, to update me of your decision, Assaf.

*

- That's it, Michal. I am out. They kicked me out of Operations. There's nothing more for me to do there.

- Don't rush into any decision. They gave you forty-eight hours to decide. Take a breath. Go down to your beach, have a quiet think. Besides, it's not all bad. Consider the silver lining: we have been considering a more peaceful life for quite some time now, and it's also high time you get to know your kids.

Long before those forty-eight hours were up Assaf walked back into the chief's office, where he was always welcome, even on short notice.

- I've decided to accept your offer.

- I'm glad. Good luck to you.

Assaf had the advantage of major budgets and top operatives, as well as the free hand to establish the new department and shape it as he saw fit. He invited delegates from the Ministry of Defense and the Foreign Office to the department's first meeting.

- We are not here to compete with the Ministry of Foreign Affairs. Rather, our job is intelligence gathering as a means to preserve Israel's safety and security as well as undermine those who wish to harm us. Mossad operated covertly, and mostly in countries the Foreign Office cannot, things being what they are, operate in.

In one fell swoop, Assaf was able to dispel years of animosity and rivalry between the Mossad and the other ministries, a hostility fueled by competition for turf, prestige and purview.

Assaf regarded improving Mossad's intelligence school and extending its international network of ties as paramount. Mossad's reputation among intelligence organizations worldwide garnered a flurry of offers of cooperation, along with requests for allowing intelligence officers the world over to enroll in

Mossad's training programs. One conclusion from all this was that whosoever graduated the Mossad's programs was sure to become a potential contact. There were more applicants than the Mossad could possibly accommodate. The admissions committee, headed by Assaf himself, comprised of delegates from the Mossad, the Foreign Office and the Ministry of Defense.

- I'd like to bring up a special issue in the framework of our meeting today," Assaf said in one of the committee's conferences. "Seeing as this is a complex matter, I allow myself to elaborate more than usual. This concerns Jeronti, a country where Israel has vast interests. Jeronti has enormous reserves of oil, on top of other natural resources, some strategically important. The country's problems stem from its social and religious structure: some thirty-six different tribes. Being a former British colony, English is their common language, but it's pretty much the only thing they have in common. Jeronti's population is equally divided between Christians and Muslims. There is a great deal of bad blood between them. The relations between Jeronti and Israel have had their ups and downs, primarily due to the tribal and religious wars there. The ministry of foreign affairs has been scrambling to operate there. Most often, difficulties stem from a conflict of interest. Mossad has a station in Jeronti. We recently came across an opportunity to expand our operations there. I would like to highlight the application we received from one of the leaders of the largest militias in Jeronti. He wants to enroll at our intelligence school. He is a Muslim, and is also opposing the central government. We shy away from intervening in any country's internal strife. Nevertheless, we have information according to which this militia is about to seize control of Jeronti, so mustn't miss this opportunity of forging closer relations with this country."

And so, the committee voted unanimously in favor of admitting Mkume Shibu into the Mossad's program.

*

That has been one of the school's most festive graduation parties. Each cadet was asked to show up wearing their national costume. Assaf himself put in an appearance in the guise of a kibbutznik, having exhausted all his creativity on secret missions. He had on khaki shorts, a Russian-farmer's shirt and open sandals. He even sported a bucket hat and a false mustache befitting Stalin, much to the delight of his students, who could not help wondering whether other Israeli secret agents had the same get-ups in mind during their actual missions.

Shibu got hold of the mic at the end of the party. Tall and handsome, wearing a white robe with golden threads and a white headdress, he greeted the Mossad and gave a toast, praising Assaf Shlomi in person. He concluded his tribute with "Shalom".

*

One day, Assaf came to see the Mossad chief.

- Good morning to you, my friend and commander. I've come to tell you I decided to retire from Mossad. I owe you a personal debt for everything you've done for me and for all the chances you have given me. Nevertheless, you know what they say, 'enough is enough'!

- I knew this day would come. I also know there's no point

trying to convince you to stay on. We will find the proper way to see you off. We shall find a replacement for you by tomorrow. Rest assured it will be a thorough transition. My regards to Michal.

- Thank you, and good luck!

Upon his retirement, Assaf signed an agreement in which he pledged not to engage in any pursuit that coincided with Mossad's activities for the following three years.

The very next day, Assaf went to a law firm, where he registered a new company, "Shlomi-ya", a consulting firm on international civil projects.

CHAPTER 5

"Don't mess with 'im, that's Dudi Dayan from Dora!"

Dora, an inner city neighborhood of Netanya, is scarcely known. There is little doubt, though, Dudi's name was obscure to anyone in the city.

- Oh, I beg your pardon, I had no idea you were sitting there.

Dudi was what you might call 'a colorful person'. A man of many contradictions: come morning, he could 'waste manage' a competitor, who's body would be found later on somewhere in the sand dunes south of Netanya, and that very afternoon send a thick envelope to some bride who was too poor to buy her own wedding dress. He owned a boutique on main street, which he used to frequent every now and then, helping a customer choose an Armani suit he had imported himself. Clothes were his personal weakness.

"Some people paint on the weekend," he used to explain to his friends, "others write for fun or play sports, but I love clothes. Shame I do not have the time to spend as much as I'd like on this hobby of mine." His words still reverberated as he went off to "attend" to some "associate" who was late paying his protection.

Dudi cut a dashing figure, sporting the most elegant clothes to compliment his strong physique and handsome features, much to the delight of Netanya's womenfolk. Assaf, his best friend, would someday explain this as "the criminal mystique": the combination of the air of the "charming mobster", a captivating leader, good looks and lavish generosity. Dudi was also highly respected by the menfolk, some of whom admired him, whereas others feared him. A real pro, he ran his own "boardwalk empire" with an iron fist and panache, fueled by the absolute confidence he exuded and his men's total obedience. It was common knowledge that loyalty was aptly rewarded, as was betrayal.

"You do not mess with Dudi!" was the common maxim around town.

The anecdote about the brazen fool who stole from Dudi was whispered in close quarters. To this day, so they say, the police have yet to collect the poor sod's entire remains. It had become commonplace for the police to have Dudi arrested first, whatever case they were working, as a matter of procedure. Figuring it wouldn't hurt the police's reputation, or undermine their investigation either, they would book him, only to have him appear, the picture of elegance, before the magistrate, ready to be arraigned. The police would then show extra care in processing him, avoiding so much as the slightest crease to his white linen shirt and shiny shoes. The rumor goes that some rooky policeman once dropped to Dudi's feet to clean a speck off one of his shoes. The magistrates too played the game, often greeting him with a smile, only to order his immediate release due to lack of evidence. Dudi would then leave court all calm and smiling, straight to his boutique. Nevertheless, some police officers still entertained the hope of securing his conviction someday.

- All rise!

Everyone at the Tel Aviv District Court's main hall rose to their feet, including people who viewed the proceedings as a spectator sport. They would never miss a good murder story. The audience naturally comprised of civil attorneys who came to see what the fuss was all about, journalists in search of tomorrow's headlines, anxious family members and the usual cackle of Dudi's female fans.

- Criminal case number two eight eight dash eight, the State of Israel vs. Dudi Dayan. Justice Yitzhak Kimhi presiding, alongside Justice Naomi Tzivion to his right and Justice Ya'akub Khamzi to his left.

The judges' clerk resumed her seat, her excitement attesting to this being her first criminal trial. Nevertheless, her apprehension at the grave responsibility she bore did not prevent her from noticing her mother's proud smile from the second row of the courtroom's aisle.

Justice Kimhi, as esteemed as he was experienced in years and procedures, turned to the peoples' bench, and asked, imposing and dignified, "are the people wishing to make their case?"

Justice Tzivion looked at the state attorney inquisitively. Much younger than her fellow justices on the bench, her fair hair and good looks earned her the spectators' favor, all the more so as she was rumored to be a rising star, with persistent news of her impending appointment to Israel's Supreme Court.

The third judge, Justice Ya'akub Khamzi, a Christian Arab, who was appointed to the Tel Aviv District Court some time earlier, was part of this panel of judges for three years now. Rather bored and aloof looking, this was the last criminal case before him prior to his retirement. He felt he had seen it all before and could hardly be surprised anymore. Consequently, this particular trial bode nothing special as far as he could see.

The attorney for the prosecution replied:

- Yes, may it please the court.

She was the district attorney's second deputy. Her second and third chair, two junior attorneys, sat right next to her. Behind the prosecution's bench, sat, alert and ready, their young interns.

Presiding over all these proceedings was Justice Kimhi. Seasoned and astute, he realized why it was that the district attorney did not try this particular case herself, or at least delegate the case to her first deputy. When you assign a case to your number three, this can mean either that the evidence stacked against the accused is so unimpeachable, that you can allow the younger attorneys gain some experience without running the risk of them botching the case, or the opposite, that the case is so flimsy, you'd better let someone else take the wrap for losing it. Either way, Justice Kimhi couldn't resist himself. He just had to share his ruminations with his fellow judge. He snuck a note to Justice Tzivion, who in turn smiled briefly and folded it back.

The deputy district attorney continued:

- May it please the court, the people hereby accuse the defendant that on Tuesday, at half past one in the afternoon, he, and another person, did shoot one Ya'akov Dahari, in broad daylight, in Netanya's main street, Independence Street, killing him within three shots. The people would therefore ask that the defendant, Dudi Dayan, be found guilty of murder in the first degree according to Article 300 in the Penal Code of 1977. The State has incontrovertible evidence to support this, inter alia, thanks to a witness who has turned state's evidence.

"Silence in the courtroom!" Justice Kimhi responded to the

hisses that greeted the people's opening statement.

- If order is not maintained, I shall clear the courtroom and resume proceedings in closed doors! Kindly proceed, madam counselor.

- The people have ample circumstantial evidence to corroborate the case against the defendant. As the indictment shows, our charges rely on some two hundred and fifty witnesses, most of whom were technical spectators at the scene, but seeing as the perpetrators wore masks at the time of the shooting, their collective testimony does not amount to much. We can consequently dispense with summoning them.

- How long do you require to make your case?

- May it please the court, Justice Kimhi, I cannot estimate the time the defense would require for cross examination, but I do believe I would probably require four hearings, maybe six at the most.

- Does the defense have a statement?

The defendant's legal team, comprising two self-conscious attorneys, whispered to one another. All too familiar with the evidence, they could hardly respond any differently:

- May it please the court, we shall respond to the actual charges, one by one, in the course of the trial.

When asked how long the defense would require to make its own case, they replied that they could neither, at that point, anticipate how long their cross examination would take, nor how long they would require to introduce their counter evidence, but they did quip that interrogating the people's witness who had turned state evidence would require numerous lengthy hearings.

At that moment, the defendant, who was until then peaceful at the dock, surrounded by four burly guards, snapped:

- I am innocent! It's all lies!

But the presiding judge was no doubt impressed with the prosecution's opening speech, for he shouted back at the defendant:

- One more disturbance and I'll have you removed!

He then proceeded to adjourn the meeting, not before scheduling ten additional hearings to hear the case out.

*

- Case 288/8, the date is October 8, Justices Kimhi, Tzivion and Khamzi presiding, the people, the defense and the defendant are all present. I hereby invite the prosecution to call its first witness.

Justice Kimhi then continued:

- Let this be a warning to the defendant, that were he to cause any disturbance during these proceedings, I shall have him removed forthwith!

The district attorney's second deputy rose up.

- I hereby call out first witness, Mordechai Nahari. Having signed an agreement to turn state evidence, he was awarded immunity of the counts of murder in the first degree, provided he testifies truthfully concerning the allegations specified against the defendant. He was further promised that all charges and open criminal cases against him shall be dropped immediately following his testimony. May it please the court, here is the letter of agreement. Opposing counselor has a copy of that, which they received during discovery. Please call Mordechai Nahari to the stand.

The first witness for the prosecution made his way to the stand accompanied by his own detail of sturdy bodyguards, but he was nevertheless trembling with fear as he fixed his eyes firmly down into the witness box as he took an oath so say nothing but the truth. He then proceeded to give his testimony:

- On Tuesday at half past one the defendant and I were on Independence Street in Netanya. When we saw Dahari coming towards us, the defendant pulled out a gun from his back pocket and shot Dahari three times.

In response to which, Dudi screamed at the top of his lungs:

- You dirty liar! I never shot anyone! I don't even know you!

The four guards assigned to the defendant pounced on him and forced him down back to his seat. Due to all this commotion, the chief magistrate called a recess and left in a hurry, together with the other two judges.

After the short break, the justices returned, having beefed up Dudi's detail with additional correctional officers.

- I would like the defense team to advise their client that should he make any further disturbances I shall be forced to conduct his own trial in his absence. The prosecution may call its first witness back to the stand!

The witness resumed his testimony under the watchful eye of three hulking guards seated at various points within the courtroom, who also kept eying the defendant.

- Immediately after the shooting, Dudi handed me the gun he used to fire at Dahari, as he told me he would the day before.

The prosecutor asked:

- What else was in your arms?"

- Right before Dudi pulled out the gun, he gave me a pair of leather gloves and put on a pair for himself as well.

- Do you happen to recall what color were those gloves?

- Yes. Khaki. Like an army uniform.

- Go on.

- Well, I took the gun from him and hid it in my own jacket pocket. I then ran up north and Dudi ran towards the beach. After about half a mile or so, I headed for the coastal road, where I descended to the underpass. I found this pile of rocks and stashed the gun there, under the rubble. I ran to the other side of the underpass and dropped both gloves in this ditch by an orange grove. Then, I ran over to the junction, hopped on a bus to Hadera and walked the rest of the way home.

- Let me show you this silver Beretta gun number k296785. Do you recognize it?

- Yeah. This here is the gun Dudi used to shoot the victim. It's the same piece I hid under the coastal road.

- How can you be so sure? What makes you identify it so definitively?

- Its grip has a slight bend down there. I can also tell by its color.

The counselor for the prosecution handed the gun to the bailiff.

- May it please the court, let the record show the people mark this gun 'Exhibit One'.

After it was so noted, she resumed the course of her questions:

- Now, do you recognize this pair of gloves?

- Yes. These look a lot like the ones I had on during the murder, which I threw into that ditch.

The prosecutor handed the bailiff the gloves and Justice Kimhi ordered they be marked as 'Exhibit Two'. Both exhibits were rewrapped up in protective plastic and returned to the file.

- Am I to understand you are through examining your witness, counselor?

- Yes, your honor.

- Then I hereby call the defense to have him cross examined.

Chief Magistrate Kimhi seemed highly pleased at the testimony, which only served to strengthen his preliminary conviction the defendant was indeed guilty of the murder. Dudi withstood two whole days of testimony and cross examination and, save for a few minor inconsistencies, he stuck to his guns and professed his innocence the entire time.

It was then police Sergeant Yitzhak Va'anunu's turn to take the stand.

- I serve at the Netanya precinct. The moment we received a report on a shootout on Independence Street, I went over to the scene, where I was ordered to look for any suspects and gather any evidence that might be related to the incident. In the course of my pursuit, I reached the emergency underpass under the coastal road. Right in the middle there, I spotted this suspicious looking pile of rubble. When I examined it, I found this silver Beretta gun, which I bagged as evidence and brought back with me.

- Here is 'Exhibit One' which I am showing you. Do you recognize it?

- Yes. This is the same gun I found at the underpass. I can tell by its number and by the bend on the grip right there, at the butt.

- This here is a pair of khaki leather gloves, marked as 'Exhibit Two'. Do you recognize them?

- Yes. This is the pair I found in the ditch.

The next witness for the prosecution was Superintendent Avi Naor from Forensics. He testified that the lab test found the gun cartridges found at the scene, along with two bullets retrieved from the body, were fired from a Beretta gun, serial number k296785.

As for the gloves, he testified they could not be used to retrieve any finger prints.

Whereas the people concluded their case, the defense consisted of one testimony, that of the defendant. He uttered the following single sentence:

- I have no idea what you people want from me. I have never killed anyone. I am innocent.

The following hearing took place a month later. The panel of judges announced they had found the defendant guilty of murder. They set the sentencing hearing for another thirty days.

Nevertheless, a week went by, and the police arrested a criminal in Be'er Sheva in suspicion of a murder that had taken place there. After intensive interrogation, he pleaded guilty and as the investigation proceeded, he later on pleaded to three additional counts of murder, including the one at Independence Street at Netanya. Israel's National Crimes Division was assigned to examine the veracity of that criminal's confession, and they soon corroborated it concerning all of the murders he indeed confessed to, including the one at Netanya. Head of Crime Investigations appointed yet another committee to look into the Netanya precinct's shameful debacle. The committee's investigators uncovered that the head of the local precinct was so firmly convinced of Dudi's complicity in the murder, he allowed himself to cut corners and even went as far as to contrive evidence. At the end of their internal investigation, he was removed from the force without trial.

The panel of judges at the Tel Aviv District Court was then summarily convened to rule in the case against Dudi. The prosecutor bowed her head in embarrassment as she pleaded his innocence and that his case be dismissed with prejudice.

The justices did not so much as glance at Dudi's defense team as they acquitted him and hurried out of the courtroom.

*

During all this time, amounting to twenty-five months, Dudi was serving his time in prison until he was summarily released. After the scene in court, he drove straight to his favorite fish restaurant, where he dined together with two close friends. He fulfilled the craving he harbored during his incarceration and relished on seared sea bass, which he washed down with draught beer.

After lunch, he went straight home near Netanya, kissed his wife and kids and told them he was going out on a two-day retreat dedicated to introspection. He indeed spent the following days by himself in a cabin on the beach, gazing at the sea and looking back at his life events. On his second evening there he reached the following conclusion: '*If I am destined to be a criminal, I might as well be a top dog*'. Those twenty-five months in custody took their toll. He was never allowed any leave and was seldom allowed to have any family visits. Once he was freed, no one apologized, nor was he even compensated for his false imprisonment. '*Now that I am doomed to be thought of as a villain,*' he thought, '*let me be a real live Kingpin*'.

Always considered intelligent, this young man was always attributed with acumen, ferocity, striking leadership skills and magnanimity - on top of being uninhibited by any moral considerations. He was a gifted decision maker, and he was also exceptional at getting things done. He summed his entire personality and experience into ten precepts, which he formulated at the beach. From that time onwards, these principles were his constant guide.

1. "*Be* **Not** *a tail to lions,* **Nor** *a head to foxes – but rather the head Lion.*" [Which he changed compared with the original maxim in Mishnah, Tractate Avot, *Ethics of the Fathers*: Chapter Four, verse 15: "*Be a tail to lions, rather than a head to foxes*".]

2. "Seek no one's protection. Never be a protégé: Be the provider of protection."

3. "Though shall not take a life: unless under threat to your person or business."

4. "Though shall not steal. Nevertheless, stealing from a thief is exempted from penalty."

5. "Always plead the Fifth: adhere to your right to keep silent."

6. "Never believe any cops, least of all nice cops."

7. "Never turn state evidence: do not accept a plea bargain."

8. "Always view the court system with the utmost suspicion."

9. "Once you're 'inside', be sure to establish your standing immediately. Never let them walk all over you."

10. "While inside, never forget the walls have ears – and the inmates, mouths."

Dudi Dayan was a born leader. Whenever Israel's top criminals convened, they always paid him the highest respect, abiding by his final word on whichever subject. His verdict was binding. His character, complete with his traits and skills, indeed propelled him to the position of supremacy in the criminal 'underworld'. A bon vivant, he was the coveted patron of many fashionable Tel Aviv restaurants and the choicest boutiques of Paris. His day to day life amounted to a detail of bodyguards and the snazziest car, which his chauffer would inspect from every angle before starting, only after which would Dudi climb in, thirty seconds into the motor's running.

"Experience is the best teacher," Dudi once told his son.

Dudi's empire grew and expanded as the years went by. His activity spanned the length and breadth of the entire country, even exceeding Israel at times. He set himself two rules: avoid drugs and embrace any adrenaline pumping adventure, for all the curiosity it afforded him.

*

Every now and then, Dudi went down to the beach he had once shared with Assaf. Their 'private' beach was strewn with slippery rocks whose green sheen was punctuated by the white sand. The rocks deterred the bathers, so the beach was secluded, much to Dudi and Assaf's delight in the solitude this afforded them, so much so that they were spared the company of strangers for days on end. Once, they discovered a tunnel under the rocks, which led to the open sea. They soon discovered that several dolphins have made the same discovery coming in from the Mediterranean. Once they were done diving for the time being, they would sit together right by the water and exchange stories, enjoying their time together and their camaraderie. But all this was a long time ago. Each of them drifted, as life often takes people onwards, each to one's own summit.

Nevertheless, Dudi has never abandoned that beach. He would go there on occasion to relax and contemplate between his dives. He never met Assaf at their beach, but still, he knew somehow that he wasn't the only person frequenting the site and that Assaf and he would meet at the tunnel again some time.

CHAPTER 6

Eli was born in Cape Town. His father, Ilan Alon, came over from Tel Aviv, but he was to remain thanks to Jackey. A diamond trader, his work brought him to South Africa quite frequently. Bored, it occurred to him to drop in, at a moment's notice, on the local Jewish country club, where he fell upon this gorgeous young woman. The rest, as they say, was history. Jackey insisted they stay in South Africa once they were married, and Ilan in turn insisted their son would bear a name similar to his own.

And so it was that Eli, who was born very soon after the marriage, became bilingual, as Alon insisted on talking to the boy in Hebrew, and Jackey stuck to her guns in English. An exceptional kid, Eli got his dark skin from his father and his big blue eyes from his mother. His courage, determination and curiosity were divine gifts. Eli traveled to Israel quite often to visit with his father's family while on holiday, and he got to know his father's homeland pretty well. He especially liked visiting his uncle at Yavne'el, very close to the Sea of Galilee, as he had a large sheep farm there. Eli loved to feed the sheep and protect them from any menacing wolf.

When he turned eighteen, he bid his mom farewell and went to Israel to join the army. Accompanied by his father, he enlisted to the Intelligence Corps, thanks to the recruitment officers' keen observation of his attributes: an inquisitive and courageous man with a good head on his shoulders with a perfect command of English.

"One plus one makes three," Eli Alon firmly believed. *'Whosoever thought otherwise,'* he thought, *'is a square, a chump towing the line'*. That's why he soon became a high flier in his unit. For instance, according to his intelligence analysis, if open and covert sources alike, on satellite imagery, human reports, surveillance and so on, all point to the conclusion war was not imminent, then it was high time, in his opinion, mind you, to replenish reserves and make sure there was plenty of ammo in the emergency stores.

Eli acquired a reputation that went far beyond the Israeli intelligence community. He was thought of as creative, highly imaginative and resourceful. The IDF made ample use of his talents, and so it was that he took part in many a secret mission involving various outfits from numerous corps. This is how he and Assaf met. There years of working together forged a friendship that transcended the difference in ages and upbringing.

Once his compulsory military service was done, Eli simply vanished for a few years. Gone without a trace, as it were. Only years later, did his friends learn he had served time in some prison in South Africa, but all attempts to find out under what circumstances met with his staunch resistance. Rumors spread he was involved in some clandestine operation down there, that went sour, landing him in jail. The Israeli authorities struck some secret deal with the South African government and secured his extradition and subsequent release to Israel, after which Eli kept his head down, until, that is, the call came from Assaf.

CHAPTER 7

Dr. Dmitry Blog felt the noose tightening round his neck. He took off the third tie he was trying on, frantically attempting to match it to his azure striped shirt, seeing as he owned only three other shirts. He couldn't shake that suffocating feeling, on top of which, he felt this uncontrollable shudder all the way down his spine.

Rushing off to her own work, Paulina looked in on him.

- What's come over you today, Dima? Who are you going to meet? Why have you got your striped shirt on? I've told you once, I've told you a thousand times, the plaid shirt looks better on you!

Slamming the door behind her, Paulina didn't wait for him to reply, as she was in a hurry. His wife of fifteen years was a certified nurse at the Ana Zbrodnevya Psychiatric Hospital at the outskirts of Moscow. Notwithstanding her demanding work, she ran their household like a tight ship.

Dima greatly appreciated his wife's intelligence and saw in her his friend, partner and shoulder. Nevertheless, her hurried departure that morning was a blessing to him, for he was at a loss as to how to open up to her about what had happened. *'What can I tell her? That I am scared to death? That I have this fatal premonition? Well, I could, maybe I should, tell her about*

*that surprise summons to the hospital chief, but now I don't have
to, seeing as she's already out the door'.*

*

Dima has been working as an anesthesiologist at Moscow's
government hospital these past seventeen years, and never
during this entire time was he ever called up to see the manager.
In fact, little did he hold out for such a meeting to ever take
place. Dima had very low expectations of himself. After his
retirement from the Red Army, having earned the rank of
Lieutenant, he considered his next course in life. Medicine
wasn't in the cards for him, he felt. Not only did he not care for
the medical profession, he did not consider himself capable
of even getting accepted on his own merit. The option of
applying to the University of Moscow's Faculty of Medicine
despite falling short of the qualifications rose only as a result
of his mother, a doctor's widow for many years, pleading and
imploring him. He finally relented and applied, but was hardly
surprised and not at all disappointed when, following months
of exams and interviews, he received the we regret to inform
you letter notifying him he did not get in. Yet, much to Dima's
shock, he received another letter from the university a while
after that, notifying him as follows:

*In light of new circumstances, the university board has decid-
ed to admit you as a medical student.*

Dima's inquiries as to the reasons for this sudden change
revealed that a few young men who did get accepted to med
school received luring offers to serve in an elite secret Red
Army unit. The candidates' decision to forego their medical
studies in favor of a promising military career freed up vacan-

cies the university opted to fill with formerly rejected candidates, one of whom was Dima himself.

His first few years in the medical faculty merely exacerbated Dima's sense that he wasn't cut out to be an MD, all the more so practice medicine. Both his social and academic interactions with his fellow students, be it at uni or when they got together to drink on occasion in between exams, underscored his feeling they were bright people with bright futures ahead of them, whereas he was muddling through somehow, with very little luster and even less talent.

By the time he was in his fifth year, Dima concluded that even if he were to graduate, all he could aspire to was the post of some family doctor in some mining town in far-off Siberia. His only alternative was to abandon his studies and look for another source of gainful employment at the age of thirty-two in the bleak Soviet labor market. But when he began his sixth year at med school, Dima came across a circular the faculty had posted, recommending a program to specialize in anesthesiology, complete with special benefits. Seeing as most medical students had little regard for the profession of an anesthesiologist, especially compared with other options, he saw his chance to securing not only a trade but also a residency at a government hospital in Moscow. And so it was that Dima applied to the anesthesiology program, as did another female student.

*

After graduation and upon receiving his credentials, Dima was appointed to the Maxim Gorky Hospital in Moscow. After another postgraduate training program, he was certified as an anesthesiologist, where he spent the following seventeen years in grueling shifts until being summoned to the manager of the hospital out of the blue.

Dima came to terms with his work surprisingly well and appreciated its positive aspects, in particular the routine that was in line with his own personality. Very few events undermined the constant flow of his duties. On one occasion, a patient came to in the middle of the operation, which was summarily cut short, giving Dima time to up the dosage of the sedatives. The investigation held following this case determined it was Dima who administered a quantity that was too low, so he received a professional reprimand that went on his permanent record. In another case, the patient did not wake up after his surgery, which was very alarming for the operating room staff. The event did eventually end on a positive note when the patient did rise and was taken to the recovery room.

Another event proved a source of grave worry for Dima. An inspection of the surgical ward uncovered a discrepancy between the hospital records and the actual quantities of anesthetics stored. The inquest into this matter found nothing, and the case was closed due to lack of any evidence.

*

And so, during all those seventeen years that Dima worked at the hospital, he was never called to see the manager. When he was summoned, the prospect literally made him queasy. Before he even got a chance to marvel at the opulence and luxury of the director's indeed lavish offices, Irena, the manager's all-powerful secretary, motioned him to hurry in. As he walked in, Dima saw this slim man with a bent back, looking about sixty, whom he recognized from the rare social occasions and meetings the hospital held. Seated in his tall manager's armchair, the hospital chief did not even bother to greet Dima in reply. Rather, Dima heard his irate notice:

- The autopsy revealed that Comrade Roman Zaydanovitch died as a result of an overdose of sedatives administered during his operation. Hospital protocol forces us to report this to the police. Also, given the deceased's VIP status, we shall also be informing the NKVD as well.

Dima was allowed no time to respond. Irena walked in the moment the manager pushed his buzzer, grabbed Dima by the arm and ushered him out.

*

One week prior to Comrade Zaydanovitch's medical procedure, Chief of Surgery Professor Yevgeny Alexandrovitch chaired the regular staff meeting at the usual scheduled time of Monday at nine o'clock. He announced that sometime in the course of the following days, a senior party figure and an important person in the country's defense establishment was to undergo an operation. Prof. Alexandrovitch added that he was not at liberty to disclose the patient's identity at that time, citing national security considerations, nor the exact date of the procedure.

*

- What is it Lina? What are all these ambulances doing at the entrance?

Lina, the chief surgical nurse, a beautiful woman in her late forties, was always well groomed. Nevertheless, that particular day, Dima barely recognized her pale and weary face.

- You're not going to believe this, Dima. They woke me up in the middle of the night and ordered me to vacate all the patients from Ward B.

- Where could you possibly take them? Even the corridors are full!

- I sent all the patients in rooms one through seven to other floors. I even put a few of them in cots in the doctors' room. I am moving the patients from rooms ten through sixteen to other nearby hospitals, which is why we've got those ambulances out front.

- And what about room eight and nine?

- We vacated them yesterday and designated these rooms off limits. We mustn't go near them.

- What have you done with Nikolai, the gut we operated on yesterday morning?

- Nikolai and the other patients who cannot be moved for fear of their lives, we're moving down the corridor, where they already assigned security guards. I saw them.

Prof. Alexandrovitch seemed highly tense that morning all throughout the meeting. Dima had never seen him in such a state. The chief surgeon, whose broad shoulders were always there for any female staff member, seemed shrunken somehow. Not only that, the professor's voice seemed to tremble.

- In addition to my previous instructions, I hereby cancel all scheduled procedures with immediate effect.

The hospital called another urgent meeting that very afternoon. Dr. Alexandrovitch seemed to have aged overnight since that morning, as he announced:

- The operation is to be held tomorrow morning. The surgical staff will be headed by Professor Moldov, who will be in charge of the procedure. Dr. Dmitry Blog will be the chief anesthesiologist. The entire medical staff, along with all the auxiliary staff, is hereby asked to remain in doors tonight, and not go out of their homes.

The morning of the surgery, Dima reported to Surgery Room One along with the rest of the extended medical staff. The operating theater was teaming with medical staff, on top of those surrounding the operating room. Dima spotted four burly men in gowns and surgical headbands at each corner.

The patient underwent a further examination, after which the team of doctors proceeded to prepare him for surgery along with the nursing staff. Dmitry then began executing the preplanned anesthesia protocol. The patient was sound asleep and ready for his operation within ten minutes.

The operation itself went well, without a hitch. Three hours and forty minutes later, when the chief surgeon was done, he retired to his room and left suturing to his assistants. When they were done, Dima and another senior member of the surgical staff remained in the room to oversee the completion of the suture stage and the sedation wearing off. Dima knew from his experience that patients usually come to about thirty minutes after their procedure is over. This phase usually takes about forty minutes. Thirty minutes into this, Dima was beginning to stress and fret. When the patient still had not woken up, Dima's distress turned to major concern. The senior doctor, however, was immersed in his magazine. Another ten minutes passed, and still no change in the patient's status, so Dima called the doctor's attention. Five minutes into their monitoring his signs, they literally sounded the emergency alarm - seeing as there was no new development.

The operating room filled with medical staff within seconds.

The hospital's top experts did their utmost to resuscitate the patient. An hour and a half later, the chief surgeon pronounced Comrade Roman Zaydanovitch dead. Every member of staff, including Dima, was completely stunned. The deceased's body was taken for autopsy, which, everyone hoped, would find that the cause of death had nothing to do with their performance. Evening came, and there was still no result, so they dispersed.

*

Dima had never thought of himself as a Jew. During his mother's last days, succumbing to her prolonged illness, she did tell him she, and therefore him, were of Jewish descent. He himself had been an atheist living in an atheist environment, so he attributed no importance to his background whatsoever. Nevertheless, his wife Paulina did raise the possibility of uprooting to Israel. Her mother wasn't Jewish, but Paulina's father was, with various relatives living in Israel, where, according to what they were telling her, life was pretty sweet. Dima dismissed the idea. He never considered, not for one moment, giving up his comfortable life and relocating to Israel, of all places.

*

A few hours had passed since Dima saw his wife off that morning, without telling her about being summoned to see the hospital chief later that day. When he finally got home, Dima called Paulina at work:

- Paulina, you just have to come home at once.

- What is it, Dimochka? You looked so fine this morning, what with that nice striped shirt and tie I got you at Arbat.

What's wrong?

He was on the verge of tears. *'How do you tell your wife her life is about to change so radically over the phone?!'*

- I am asking you to please come early this evening. I cannot discuss this over the phone.

- I've got a lot of work, but all right, I promise. Mwah.

Her gesture of "mwah" kisses over the phone and her promise to return home early were just what Dima needed to calm himself down. The temporary relief afforded him some time on his own, which he used to think things through. He sat at his favorite spot at home, a large vodka right next to him, and analyzed the course of events. Eventually, he came to the conclusion that Israel was the only way out of his predicament.

*

Paulina came home that afternoon, tempestuous as an autumn early breeze. She kissed Dima on his forehead. He breathed in her scent, which was a mixture of body odor and all sorts of pharmaceuticals, clean sheets and detergents.

- See, Dimochka? Early, just as I promised!

The man she now saw before her was in no way the Dima she had left that morning. All throughout their marriage, he had never looked this beaten and stricken. It did not take her a second to figure out something terrible was up.

- What's wrong, Dimochka?

Paulina's racing train of thought circled the globe, running from some malignant illness he was diagnosed with to, G-d forbid, something involving their daughter.

- Unless you want me all bagged up, get packing!

His outburst and crying came as a complete shock to her.

She couldn't believe it was coming from him.

This once proud Red Army officer, a successful doctor and he-man, has suddenly turned into this mush of misery. So much so, that he was beside himself. '*I do recall he did tell me yesterday morning, when I was in a hurry about to leave for work, late as usual, that he was going to be part of an important operation that day*'. She did hear, but she didn't really listen, as such procedures are part of his daily routine. She did pay attention, though, when he promised they would go to their favorite restaurant on Wassiliski Sposek Street that evening, but then they had to take a raincheck due to the hospital directing the staff to remain at home for the evening and night ahead of that all-important surgery the following day, to make sure they were well rested. '*Dima did mention something about an important event this morning as well, I think*,' but she was more focused on what he was wearing, that shirt she had bought him once at Arbat, when she felt particularly uplifted, completely unaware of his perplexity.

Paulina cared for only one thing more than she did her work and her husband: shopping for clothes. She would spend what little spare time she had trotting up and down central Moscow's shopping district, in particular Arbat Prospect and Evropeisky Mall. Every now and then, she would take Dima along to the Izmailovsky Flea Market on a Sunday. The pride of many a Muscovite, often referred to, with more than a touch of local patriotism, this is the world's largest and most diverse venue for shopping, where they would indeed supplement their wardrobe with items they could not otherwise afford, given the prices at Moscow's high-end department stores.

Paulina caressed her husband's hair, handed him a glass of cold water and asked softly:

- So what is, Dimochka?

It took him quite a while to pull himself together before he could reply.

- The patient from yesterday's surgery died on the operating table. They say it was due to some failure with the anesthetics.

'*Oh, so it's not some terrible illness or something to do with our family*,' Paulina felt relieved.

- I'm terribly sorry, but these things do happen. Everyone knows you're an expert doctor, so out of thousands of operations, a few are bound to turn out not so well.

Rather than calm down, Dima burst out crying once again.

- You don't see. The patient was a senior commander in one the security services.

Paulina's complacency began to unravel.

- That's truly disconcerting. But then again, what could possibly happen?

- I was told the NKVD is in the picture. They are about to come for me at any moment, for all I know.

- But surely you can prove this was a mistake of some kind. You didn't do it on purpose.

Paulina was finally beginning to grasp the gravity of the situation.

- No way. The secret police have to show some result for their efforts, so they'll have me arrested in no time. I am the only person they could pin this on.

With this, he collapsed altogether. He cried uncontrollably and was shaking all over.

- They can ship me off to some gulag in Siberia, put me away for many years, and that's the best-case scenario.

Paulina felt like her entire world was caving in. She immediately realized her well-to-do existence was falling apart.

- So what are you going to do?

Dima noticed she wasn't referring to the situation as a mutual problem, but rather his own.

- I came to the following decision: I found there's a flight that's leaving tonight at midnight. I'll book me one seat on the Austrian Airlines flight to Vienna. Assuming they still haven't filed a stay of exit order against me yet, I plan on boarding this flight.

- And what are you going to do in Vienna?

- Find a connection to Israel. I'll take another flight. I'm sure my cousins in Israel will help me get settled.

The more Dima elaborated on the situation and on his plans, he regained his self-confidence. Conversely, Paulina receded into herself in fear and desperation.

- What will become of me and Masha?

- You know how much I love you two and how hard it's going be for me to part with you, but under these circumstances, you and her had better stay in Moscow for the time being. I'm sure that tomorrow morning, when they discover I didn't show up for work, they'll come asking questions, some of which might be very unpleasant. But since you really had nothing to do with it, they will leave you be. My aim is to prepare us all a nice home in Israel and bring you and Masha over when I get a chance. Now, quit your crying and help me pack. There's not much time left.

Packing was the easiest bit. Dima had put together hand luggage he could use as his carry-on bag, inside which he carefully hid his medical kit, which he never parted with, added a few toiletries and two books from his side of the bed. Paulina folded him three of the shirts she had bought him on various occasions, to which she added two ties. In a moment's flash, she decided to keep her favorite tie, the one she got him at Evropeisky for his birthday, to herself. She added a few more undergarments, and presto. She couldn't help thinking about the amount of packing she would have to get through when her time would come.

Dima removed two thousand US dollars from some hidden location, which he had saved for a rainy day, and handed her one thousand. He neatly secreted the remaining thousand deep inside the front pocket of his pants, mindful of Moscow's expert pickpockets.

*

- Don't forget my present!

- Oh Dima, how could I possibly forget?

It was a lovely day. It was only last Sunday. The two of them went to the Izmailovsky Flea Market. Lighthearted as the sun shone. Passing through the huge fresh produce section, where plump Russian peasant women displayed their wares, they went on to the lush fruit section, sporting a bewildering spread from across Asia, from Turkey to the Far East. From then on, Paulina and Dima went over to their favorite section, the art fair, displaying the works of many and varied artists and artisans, in particular handmade jewelry by Russian and Asian craftsmen, including Uzbeks, Chinese, Tatars, Turks and so on.

- I've got a surprise for you!

This was hardly a surprise. Paulina knew Dima would never miss her present, which happened to be that week. She knew he was sure to get her a worthy gift. And so it was. He led her by the hand through the market's meandering causeways until they arrived at this brick stall so similar to many others, where, behind the old stone wall separating the market from the residential area, across the old wooden desk, this elderly man with a white beard, an Uzbek or Tajik, Paulina never could tell them apart, lit up when he glimpsed Dima.

The old man beamed as he recognized her husband. The desk had all sorts of tools lying around, from chisels, small hammers, screwdrivers, glassware filled with multicolored stones, magnifying glasses and so on.

- Are you ready?

To which the old artisan reacted by cowering over and producing this iron box from some bottom drawer. He unlocked it using a key he pulled out from his inside pocket. He opened it somewhat theatrically and laid the contents on this piece of felt. Paulina was awe struck by the most beautiful piece of jewelry she had ever seen. This was a dark blue sapphire expertly inlaid within a silver octagon. Such delicate, exquisitely tender handiwork. She watched in disbelief, admiring how it perfectly matched her eyes. So much so, it seemed to have been carved from them. The old jeweler took such pleasure with her obvious excitement, almost as much as he loved the piece he had fashioned. After all the excitement, Dima recounted his arduous walks for weeks in search of the perfect gift to match her reaching a round number of years. He told her how he eventually arrived at this Uzbek silversmith, a famous jeweler and an expert inlayer, who had obtained the precious stone from an art dealer who is an expert in special sapphires. The stone, Dima added, came from a mine in Sri Lanka. Very few mines have such stones.

Paulina chose to augment the jewelry she was so taken with. She asked to have it mended with a safety attachment to a chain, so she could secure it well. The jeweler told her it would be ready within a few days. So off she and Dima went.

- How shall I forget this beautiful sapphire you gave me? Such an amazing present?

She could not help her tears.

- My taxi is waiting.

Their parting was as hurried as it was unusual. Dima rushed out to catch his ride.

*

- I arrived safely. The family picked me up from the airport and brought me over to stay with them. They are taking very good care of me. Love and kisses to Masha.

Even before they said their goodbyes, Dima explained to Paulina it would not be wise to prolong their conversations unduly over the phone.

A few days after coming over to Israel, Dima moved to an Ulpan, a special guesthouse for immigrants where one stays during the duration of his or her Hebrew course. It was situated a few blocks from his cousin's place. Two weeks into his relocation, he had already met the chief of the Mazor Hospital. Aptly named, for '*mazor*' means 'cure' in Hebrew, this was a first rate hospital. In the course of his interview, Dima presented his credentials and certifications and recounted his medical experience. He did not spare the manager the story of his hurried flee from Moscow, along with the events that led up to it. The interview concluded with the director telling Dima how much they needed anesthetists and offered his assistance in securing Dima with a license to practice as an anesthesiologist in Israel. They also concluded that Dima will begin working there the moment he completes his Hebrew course.

Dima's transition was as fast as it was thorough. His rapid absorption was aided by the warm welcome of the medical staff, many of whom came from the former Soviet Union themselves. Dima kept in touch with Paulina on a daily basis, fueled by their hope of an impending reunion.

One day, Dima was called to see the hospital's manager. He couldn't help being overcome by recent memories on the way and dreaded the meeting. When he came, he was greeted by another man. The hospital chief invited Dima to sit across from him as he poured him a glass of water. The other gentleman introduced himself.

- My name is Gabriel. There's a number of things I would like to discuss with you."

Dima felt the familiar chill creeping down his back.

"I have a feeling you two do not need me for this," the manager exclaimed smiling as he left his own office.

Gabriel's calm smile reassured Dima, as did his gracious demeanor.

- I work for one of Israel's security forces. I heard what a fine doctor you are from the hospital chief, as well as that you're a discrete person who can keep a secret. We also did some background checks of our own. We are even familiar with Paulina and your lovely Masha. In the course of our operations, we occasionally require a doctor's assistance. We are particularly short of anesthesiologists.

- And what am I supposed to do, exactly?

- We don't have anything specific at the moment, but we'd be happy to have your consent to be part of our pool of experts. You'd be serving your country.

- But of course, no question. If you had me checked out, you must be aware of my debt to the State of Israel.

Gabriel and Dima shook hands firmly and parted.

From then on, Dima was called up to serve and avail himself of his expertise. He did not need to be informed that his services rendered were top secret and that he was not to mention any of that to a living soul. He didn't even discuss this with himself.

CHAPTER 8

One might expect that given his expertise and unique line of business, John Henry Byrot, Esq. would establish his practice at Chancery Lane, seeing as this was the heart of the City of London, home to dozens of law firms. Nevertheless, anyone who actually knew him would hardly expect his chambers to be situated there. Rather, his business address was No. 34 Bailey St., where, on the fourth floor, his was the third room on the left, at the end of a dreary corridor. Save for a faded plaque under the front door buzzer, nothing could attest this was the headquarters of one of London's top solicitors, a foremost authority on tax havens, catering to a select clientele. Byrot was intimately familiar with each and every 'offshore' financial center where he could earn his clients the best possible rerun on their deposits. As odd as it may sound, he served a mere dozen of clients. It was a special privilege to be a client of his. One had to have a minimal capital of one hundred million dollars US, on top of Byrot's personal interview and a vacancy turning up on his exclusive list.

Byrot's clients had no knowledge as to how he went about his business. All they did know was that once he received their funds, he reallocated and channeled them through intricate and separate routes that could not be traced. They also knew two additional things for sure: that the returns he fetched them were far higher than any other agent could match throughout the financial sector, and that his was a one man operation. He had in his employment only one secretary, the loyal and most trustworthy Rosaline. Even she had no clue as to who any of the clients could be, let alone the breakdown of their accounts or any other detail that may lead to their identity.

This wasn't always the case. Attorney Byrot once boasted dozens of clients who sought to stow their funds away, among whom were Persian Army officers, who turned a handsome profit from each arms deal their country was involved in. They diverted whatever commission they took to secret accounts the world over. Byrot handled some of these accounts through a contact of his, who served as a trustee. Many officers were later executed in the wake of Iran's Islamic revolution in 1979. Much to Byrot's surprise, shortly after the revolution broke out, various accounts, known only to himself and that trustee, were being liquidated. Coupled with additional warning signs, and being always the shrewd attorney, he became concerned as to his method of doing business. He suspected some strange activity was going on around him. Although he could not get to the bottom of what it was, he nevertheless sensed it was closing in on him. At the height of all this, highly weary of anything in his immediate vicinity, Byrot was summoned to Britain's Ministry of Justice.

John Henry Byrot, Esq. had never encountered any trouble with the law, let alone in his own country. He always adhered to the strict letter of the law and made a point of it. He was 'called for tea', his hosts' way of letting him know it was a friendly meeting. Following the customary exchange of pleasantries and the serving of the finest tea in the most exquisite china, he was told they initiated the parley out of concern for his own safety. The British government had received word that Iran's Revolutionary Guard had its own network of informants, an intelligence gathering effort, in fact, designed to trace funds estimated at dozens of billions of dollars that had been smuggled out of Iran by the former, now ousted regime. The chaps working on behalf of the Secretary of State for Justice came across Byrot's name on the list of the Iranian agents and saw fit to call his attention to this fact. He heeded their warning and indeed modified his modus operandi: he decided to be more selective of his clients, scrutinize them and handle no more than a dozen. This afforded him complete control over the management of their accounts, as well as enabled him to further strengthen security.

Attorney Byrot used the known tax havens: the Cayman Islands, Panama, the British Virgin Islands, the Seychelles, Jersey, and so on. He had a representative in each of these locations in the form of a local lawyer, whom he always selected very carefully, having made thorough inquiries and receiving the proper references. Byrot always made sure the attorney in his employ would possess a law degree from Britain, which guaranteed they had common ground wherever English laws were concerned, in particular a mutual understanding of England's legal and financial culture. Each of these attorneys listed dozens of front companies per Byrot's explicit instructions. The shares of these front companies were held in full by each of those local attorneys, who had exclusive signature rights, which they used to open accounts worldwide, including Andorra and Vaduz, Zurich, Balboa and even London itself. Byrot was the sole beneficiary of those accounts. He managed them through a list of codes he was in sole possession of. He made sure they were active rather than dormant, knowing all too well a dormant account is subject to scrutiny and tighter control compared with active accounts.

Byrot made customary annual visits to each of his representatives worldwide, designed to maintain their ties, touch base and test the system's secrecy. Among these tax havens, Panama City was his favorite. The local business culture made it easy to operate in the global capital markets, which suited his needs. Panama was home to hundreds of local banks, as well as local branches of the world's leading banks. On top of that, Panama had scores of law firms that knew how to conduct business and navigate through local regulations. The simplicity with which one could register a company, and the numerous legal means to mask the owners' identity, were the main qualities that drew in droves of investors the world over, keen to find a safe and discrete venue for their funds as well as their identity.

Attorney Carlos Carlotta was a relatively new associate of Byrot. When he had decided to expand into Panama City, Byrot was in the market for a local lawyer he could trust, on top of being familiar with the intricate facets of the local business scene. Byrot had in mind someone who also had sound acumen and perfect command of English. Not wishing to be indebted to the establishment, he decided to forego any references from the British Embassy. An English colleague of his eventually recommended Carlotta, citing they went to law school together back in England. That colleague earned his law degree at Oxford, so Byrot held a series of meetings with said Carlotta, after which he concluded this was indeed the right guy for him. He decided to make him his trustee and contact in Panama City.

*

"Panama City has no fewer gourmet restaurants than London," Carlotta boasted.

Byrot was sitting in Carlos Carlotta's lavish office on the thirty-second floor of an extravagant office tower near Panama City's Plaza De La Independencia. The building's northern and western walls were made of glass. One side was overlooking the Pacific Ocean in all its splendor, along with the southern part of the canal. Another window sported the sight of the city's skyline, a bustling symbol of its unique vibrancy.

This wasn't Byrot's first visit to Carlotta, but it was his first time at the attorney's new office. Much to Byrot's surprise, Carlotta placed his chair to the back of the wondrous, immersive landscape, so Byrot sat facing the views, taking them in wholeheartedly.

- Today, I am going to take you someplace special. You cannot find its equivalent in London, I assure you.

- I'd be delighted. But before we go, please explain this to me. Why are you seated with your back to the ocean, not being able to watch all these glorious sights?

- I did face the view at first. But then, I realized how much of a distraction it proved. I discovered it was better to have my guests distracted by it rather than me. Believe me, it's better for business this way.

As they left the building, Byrot saw this luxury car parked by the entrance, complete with a uniformed chauffer.

- Let's walk. It'll get our appetite going.

Carlotta discharged his driver and instructed him to wait for them by the restaurant. He then proceeded to lead his guest to Avenida Peru, Panama City's highly decorative boulevard on the marvelous oceanfront. After walking for about thirty minutes, they arrived at this enormous yet rather derelict structure, which Carlotta knew his guest would take a shine to:

- Panama City's fish market!

Byrot himself wasn't that much of a bon vivant. Back in London, the odd lunch at some run of the mill English restaurant was quite enough for him, with the occasional Indian for the sake of variety. When work was mounting, fish and chips from a nearby stand sufficed him. Though he seldom dined at renowned restaurants, he did appreciate a good meal.

Carlotta's meetings with Byrot in London were the epitome of British business-minded coldness, with the both of them having to clear a great deal of matters, so time had to be well spent on getting that out of the way, leaving no time whatsoever for any personal ties. Byrot never invited Carlotta over, and the latter knew nothing about his English host's marital status. On Carlotta's last visit to London, Byrot decided to take him to a nearby English Pub, where, after a few cold beers, he did share with his Panamanian colleague he never married, citing "never had the time". Carlotta told him he had married twice and that he has children by his first marriage. Byrot took the opportunity to tell his guest how much he was looking forward to his annual visit to Panama, "to escape the London cold."

- Don't worry. When you come to Panama City, I promise you sun, warmth and a culinary experience the likes of which you've never had.

Byrot was indeed taken aback by the local fish market, complete with hundreds of stalls. The variety of dazzling colors and the flurry of sea creatures the likes of which Byrot had indeed never seen before made quite an impression. Never ending piles of shrimps, scallops, crabs, scampi, calamari and all sorts of creatures he could not make out, as far as the eye could see, with the fresh scent of seawater and fish everywhere. Byrot relished the fishmongers' yelling at the top of their lungs and the crowds, marveling at the way the shoppers felt the wares and haggled. Many corners had young men with special-looking knives, cutting surprisingly accurately, even pieces of fresh goods, which they would throw into containers at their feet.

- What are they doing?

- Their making our ceviche.

Byrot didn't know what that was, but his London ego counseled silence rather than being thought of as ignorant. Carlotta held him by the arm and said, "Time for lunch."

Byrot did notice very early on that the entire square at the entrance to the fish market was filled with street restaurants where so many people were gorging on sea food and fish. '*Is that what he has in mind for me? Am I in for beer and sea food with all that lot?*' he wondered. Nevertheless, he soon realized he had the wrong impression, as Carlotta pulled him aside, making their way among the diners to eastern part of the market, to a staircase leading up to this terrace overlooking the whole square. They sat at one of the tables that comprised the terrace fish bodega.

As soon as they sat, this tall, brown guy pounced on Carlotta with hugs and kisses complete with Spanish greetings. Carlotta somehow managed to squeeze an introduction in.

- Meet Jogass, the owner and an old friend of mine.

A waiter appeared from nowhere, set down bottles of stiff Panamanian cerveza and turned to them in Spanish.

- He's inviting us to come down to the market to choose our main course.

Byrot, Carlotta and the waiter went down the staircase back to the market, where the waiter led them through the mountains of fish and other seafood.

- He's asking us what we would prefer to have for lunch.

Byrot's knowledge of fish didn't go any further than the fish and chips shop near his London office. That was hardly something to go by in this spectacular market.

- I can tell the waiter is a real professional, so I leave it to him to decide on the menu.

When Carlotta translated his reply, Byrot could tell how excited the waiter was, how moved by the honor he showed him, and most of all, in awe of the task. The waiter addressed him, through Carlotta, and thanked him for his confidence, vowing to rise to the challenge.

And so they left the waiter there and went back up the stairs to their table, where Jogass was already waiting. After he helped them to their seats, he gave another waiter a queue to serve them this great colorful dish with aromas that were strong as they were fine, the likes of which Byrot has never encountered. Jogass filled his plate using a large spoon and said: "you are most welcome to sample the best ceviche in the whole world."

After taking in the first taste, Byrot let the most wonderful sensation spread inside him. He had had a few delightful culinary experiences before, but this was by far the most uplifting, exciting even, feeling resulting from having food. His thrills usually derived from complex business dealings, shrewd financial moves, intricate webs he spread in tax havens, opening bank accounts and closing them, as well as other similarly 'spiritual' endeavors. It never occurred to him, not for one moment, that a colorful dish smelling so strongly like the nearby ocean would send him gushing and vibrating like that, seeing as until then, high finance was Byrot's entire world. The course he was served was as rich in taste as it was diverse in color, full with tastes of the sea, as its aromas suggested, complete with sweet and savory qualities. After he was done, his eyes spoke of his longing for more. But Jogass interjected, "You'd better slow down, as there's a lot more where that came from."

Byrot couldn't help paying him a compliment once he recovered from the jolt to his taste buds.

- What a marvelous dish! Could you tell me what I just had?
- Ceviche.

Carlos replied in Jogass's turn. He went on to explain that ceviche originated in South America, but it has become Panama's national dish.

- But what's it made of?

Jogass's face turned sour. Then, he donned a mysterious look. "I already told you Jogass's ceviche is the best in the world. All I am prepared to say, as a special favor to you to, my good friend, is that what you just had was made of twelve different kinds of seafood in a special marinade whose exact recipe I share with no one, not even my closest family. It will only be revealed in my will.

Jogass didn't even get a chance to enjoy his guests' response before two waiters emerged from the kitchen with large plates featuring all the market's produce from down below. Byrot availed himself of each and every piece, leaving no morsel untouched, and proceeded to wash it all down with the very same strong local beer they had before.

Carlotta had to prop Byrot down the stairs and help him walk over to the car that was waiting for them. The chauffer opened the door to Byrot and drove him back to his hotel.

A short while later, he drove him to the airport, where Byrot took the red eye flight back to London.

Right before he nodded off in his business class seat, Byrot wondered whether there could be some connection between that journey of culinary delights Carlotta guided him through that afternoon and his previous haphazard assertion right before that, about how he got used to have his guests face the breathtaking and distracting view of the Pacific Ocean. The thought continued to plague him until his eyes closed, as well as when he touched down in London. The thought kept bothering him over the following few days.

*

Per Byrot's instructions, Carlotta registered a firm called Paradiso among the dozens of companies he had listed in Panama City's business bureau. The company's 5,000 shares were placed in Carlotta's trust. He then transferred them to another fiduciary, an attorney from the Cayman Islands, who in turn funneled them to yet another trustee: Byrot himself. Upon its establishment, the company opened up an account at the Bank of Panama, as well as another account at the Bank of Scotland branch in the Cayman Islands. At this branch, Attorney Byrot has exclusive signatory rights. He controlled the account using a highly complex set of codes known only to him.

*

One day, Biko told Byrot he was about to receive no less than one hundred million US dollars. Byrot furnished him with the details of the Panama bank account and instructed him to transfer the money there. The very following day, Biko told him the funds had been transferred to the Panama City bank. Byrot waited for it to be morning there in order to check in with Carlotta. His phone call went unanswered, as did all subsequent attempts that day. Byrot kept stressing over the magnificent views from the thirty-second floor and the taste of ceviche. He booked a flight for that very afternoon from Heathrow to Panama City.

Immediately upon his arrival, Byrot hopped on a cab to Plaza De La Independencia and wanted to go straight up to the thirty-second floor. But he first had to go through the lobby. He went over to the receptionist:

- I am here to see Attorney Carlos Carlotta.

The guy at the desk looked at all the paperwork in front of him.

- There's no such attorney here, sir.

- What do you mean?! I was already here, at this building, only a few weeks ago. I would like to go up to the thirty-second floor, please.

- I am sorry, as I just told you, there is no attorney by that name in the entire building. Besides, you cannot go up without an invitation.

A rolled up twenty-dollar bill quickly solved that hitch. Nevertheless, there was no sign of Attorney Carlotta. The entire floor was taken up by a firm whose heavy office door had the following copper plaque: "The Panama and Central America International Investment Co."

Byrot leaned on the buzzer and was allowed into this lavish lobby, complete with thick carpeting and bowls full of fresh flowers. Over by the front red beech desk he saw this gorgeous secretary.

- Sir, how may I help you?

- I am looking for Attorney Carlos Carlotta.

- Oh, I am so sorry. Our legal department is over in another building at Avenida Peru.

- But three months ago I saw Attorney Carlotta here, on this floor!

- I am truly sorry, there is no attorney here by the name Carlos Carlotta. There are no lawyers here at all. We moved into the premises about two months ago and opened for business only a month ago, after renovating the place. Besides, as sir can see, I am very busy.

Byrot proceeded to take a taxi from Plaza De La Independencia to Bank of Panama's central branch on America Boulevard, where he had been with Carlotta, who introduced him to the bank manager with great airs. Byrot approached the receptionist and asked to see the manager.

- The manager of the bank does not see anyone without a prior appointment, sir. I do not see sir's name on the ledger for today.

- Kindly tell him I am Attorney Byrot from London. He must know who I am. You may also remind him I was here only three months ago, along with Attorney Carlos Carlotta.

The secretary spoke in Spanish over the phone and got back to him.

- The manager's office is telling me he doesn't know who sir is. I also regret to tell you they have never heard of Attorney Carlotta either. If sir is interested, I could set up an appointment to see the manager, but not in the coming two weeks, as he is leaving for his vacation in the Caribbean.

Byrot looked at the secretary's stern face and glimpsed at the burly security guards by the elevator that led to the management floor. He realized he wasn't going to find any recourse there.

"Take me to the British Consulate at Centro," he told the cab driver who pulled up next to him on the street.

The British consul was very nice. Upon receiving Byrot's calling card, he responded:

- Yes, I heard about you, but I have never heard about this Carlos chap, what did you say his full name was?

Byrot recounted his story, to which the consul replied as follows:

- Look here, the Panamanians adhere to very strict rules of caution, so meeting a bank manager is hardly a small feat. Nevertheless, through my contacts at the Bank of Panama, I might just be able to help.

He made a few calls and got back to Byrot.

- I looked into this and discovered the bank manager is fairly new. He really has never met you before, because he still hadn't been working there months ago. He has never heard of an attorney by the name Carlos Carlotta. He is not at liberty to disclose any details concerning bank accounts and money transfers, but he did hint he had never heard your name, nor about the other lawyer either.

- So what do I do?

- I really do not know what to tell you. If you'd like, let me give you the name of this detective agency we work with.

Byrot received the contact details and left the consul's office. As soon as he was out the door, he decided this was not the right place to play along with the establishment, even when it comes to the British government. He called a colleague of his from a pay phone and asked him, without elaborating too much, to furnish him with the contact details of an agency in

Panama. The colleague called him back within a few moments and off Byrot went. Over at the investigator's office, he met this bored looking gentleman seated at an empty desk.

- Hello, I am the manager here. How may I help you?

- Well, I am a businessman from England, looking to establish some business here in town. I'd like you to find a local attorney by the name Carlos Carlotta for me and to compile a case against him.

The investigator seemed keen to receive the business, all the more so as his client never haggled about the fee, twenty thousand dollars US, which he paid, upon being promised the work shall be completed speedily.

*

Byrot returned to the airport and called his London office from the business lounge. Rosaline told him she set up an appointment with the governor of the Bank of England the following day.

Byrot loved those transatlantic flights aboard British Airways, as they allowed him to disengage completely for long hours and afforded him the quality time he required to think and relax. Nevertheless, this time round, the looming sense of debacle haunted him until he landed. He even dreaded meeting the governor, whom he had never met before and was not familiar with in person.

As soon as he landed, Byrot rushed home to freshen up and continued straight to his office. Before he had a chance to reunite with Rosaline and kiss her on both cheeks, as he would always do whenever he returned from his business trips overseas, she put call through to him from Panama City.

- Hello Mr. Byrot. I'm calling you from the detective agency. I regret to inform you that due to being unforeseeably swamped with work, we couldn't possibly do the work for you. We have already instructed the bank to issue you a refund in full against the payment you've already made.

'*Evidently, I cannot trust any South American detective agencies,*' Byrot thought. He traced this agency in Miami Beach through the help of friends. That office specialized in financial investigations in South and Central America in particular. He placed a call to the manager and explained what he wanted investigated. Byrot also asked him to look into possible ties between Attorney Carlotta and Bank of Panama. The agency was all too happy to take the case and named their fee: two hundred thousand dollars US. They further concluded they will be putting through a written agreement, after whose approval and a deposit they shall began working the case.

Three days later, Byrot received a call from the head of the detective agency, who told him:

- Things are far more complicated than we had thought. We must meet in person.

They arranged to meet at the agency's offices in Miami Beach at a later date.

PART TWO

CHAPTER 9

- Two billion, three hundred and fifty million US dollars! Just bring them to me!

- Where could I possibly find such a huge sum, your Excellency, Mr. President?

- Bwana Biko, that's where! He's got it!

The luxurious desk at President Mkume Imru's was made of dark mahogany. It was surrounded by twelve armchairs with alligator skin seats. Over by the sitting corner he kept a huge bowl of fruit, from sliced pineapple through to lychee and mango to coconut dipped in honey, on top of other fragrant fruit. Next to them, coffee and tea, right next to fresh pastries. Whoever was in charge of the president's office was certainly an authority on spoiling the guests.

Mkume Shibu, head of the president's office, sat there, his spirits very low. He knew all too well the president was not to be defied.

- What are my authorities in this matter?

- You surprise me. I'm concerned, Shibu. You never ask such questions before. Do whatever it takes as long as we get the money that's coming to us.

- How long have I got?

- Three months, beginning today. Now, get to it and prove to me the old Mkume Shibu I used to know hasn't changed.

*

Seated at the head of the table and wearing a white silk robe with azure thread and a turban with white streaks, Mkume Shibu asked:

- What do we know about Bwana Biko?

The new head of intelligence, Lt. General Abdullahi, was sitting on his right, wearing his best uniform, complete with shiny buttons. Although he assumed office barely a few months earlier, he already boasted a full chest of gilded medals, gilded shoulder stripes with threads and held a wide brim hat with an orange rim.

- We all know what Biko's post was in the previous government. He was one of the most influential ministers. So much so, he often set its course. In fact, Biko was at the very top of our list of suspects. We were about to ask him a few questions about the workings of the previous government, in particular about his own role in it. We issued an order preventing his departure out of the country the moment we came to power, a decree which we disseminated throughout all border checkpoints. I regret to say that he somehow managed to receive word of our coup in advance and crossed the border between Jeronti and Benin the day before, dressed as a priest. He managed to disappear. What do you want from him?

- In a minute. Tell me, your Excellency, Finance Minister, how close was Biko to the oil revenues?

Finance Minister Mgule Kibu, another new presidential

appointee, was wearing a gray striped suit. One could immediately tell that was the work of a fine tailor from London's Bond Street. He also had on very expensive bifocal glasses.

- Biko could not be closer to these funds, as he had the most intimate relations with the international energy conglomerates. Our inquiry turned up a discrepancy of billions of dollars between what the country was supposed to receive from our oil exports and the actual proceeds of those sales.

- And what have you done with this information?

- Our inquiry has yet to be finalized. Nevertheless, I did disclose the figures to the president in our recent meeting the other day. On that same occasion, I also told him we have evidence that Biko accrued about two billion, three hundred and fifty million dollars over the years.

Shibu's dissatisfaction with the fact that Minister Kibu met with the president without his knowledge was quite apparent.

- Where did he go after he fled to Benin?

Abdullahi replied without hesitation:

- He crossed the border and went to Lomé, the capital and took a KLM flight to Amsterdam. His final destination was London.

- We know for sure that's where he is currently residing?

- Yes.

- Do we have his exact address?

Well, even if we do not, I'm sure our people at the embassy in London will be able to trace it in no time.

- OK, I heard you. We have two months to track Biko down, retrieve all the funds he stole to Jeronti and have him brought to trial for betraying the country and embezzling public funds. Ideas? Anyone?

Justice Minister Jim Rulamo, clad in a three-piece suit and

sporting a black tie, the kind litigators appear in court with, interjected:

- We have to look into our extradition treaty with England. As much as I doubt whether the funds have been deposited in any English banks, one may safely assume they were funneled to secret bank accounts in all sorts of tax havens. This would pose quite a problem tracking the money and retrieving it.

- You lawyers always complicate matters. I couldn't care less about secret bank accounts or tax havens. The president gave us all an order. It shall be obeyed to the letter. Each of you is to come up with an idea as to how we retrieve the money. We'd better come through, for all our sakes.

Governor of the Bank of Jeronti Dr. Shlibe Mngushe raised his hand, signaling he would like to add something.

- I can use my ties with the head of the Bank of England and ask his assistance in locating these funds and having them returned to us.

- Get to it, then. All of you! And remember what I said: we must not fail.

The meeting dispersed.

CHAPTER 10

Dr. Shlibe Mngushe, chief of Jeronti's central bank, had served in that position for many years. A native of Golasa, the capital, he was born into a rich family famous for its plantations of palm trees on the Niger River Delta. Their wealth stemmed from palm oil and petroleum alike. Dr. Mngushe's family never lost sight of the importance of education. Once he graduated Golasa University with a double major in economics and law, they sent him off to the London School of Economics, which he graduated with honors. His doctoral thesis, entitled "Oil and Politics in Africa", won him academic respect. His studies and long stay in London also earned him numerous skills and a profound expertise vis-à-vis the global financial markets, with a particular panache for the City of London's highly intricate financial scene. He made many friends among key legal and financial figures and did not shy away from turning said relations to his family's advantage on numerous occasions. He also assisted many a businessman on the side, as well as a succession of Jeronti's governments as a whole and key members thereof. Consequently, it was only natural he was offered the post of Governor of the Central Bank when the position became vacant. Having won the trust of one government after another, his international reputation didn't hurt his standing either. He was a frequent guest lecturer at international forums on Africa in general and oil in particular, most notably UN sponsored events. His personal reputation and cache, his professional authority and international standing combined afforded him the kind of immunity and stability in the framework of Jeronti's otherwise highly unstable political system. He managed to retain his position under any and all regimes.

Dr. Mngushe was very fond of those meetings with the president. He was among the precious few who could truly say, hand over heart, he had never sullied his hands with corrupt funds. From his own experience, he knew all too well a corrupt government cannot manage the economy well, so a corrupt country is always doomed to fall. He nevertheless kept this insight to himself, being equally aware that launching a war on corruption would soon mean his own days in office were numbered. And so he worked to the best of his abilities and hoped for the best. His meeting with Shibu gave him some encouragement that things might be headed for a change.

The day after he met Shibu, the president summoned Dr. Mngushe for another meeting, during which he told the governor the following:

- During the meeting yesterday, you told Shibu you have a few contacts back in England. Go on, then. Put your money where your mouth is. By all means, go to England, talk to whomever you think can help, and bring me the money.

CHAPTER 11

The buzzer went off on the desk of Sir Bernard McLeigh. He welcomed the pause from one of the most tedious reports from the European Central Bank.

"A 'Dr. Mngushe' wishes to see you. He is requesting two hours of your time," said Liz, Sir McLeigh's office manager.

- Who is he? Since when can I spare two hours to meet anyone, even doctors?

- He said he's the governor of the bank of Jeronti. He also told me he went to the London School of Economics with you.

McLeigh did remember the LSE, as did his fellow graduates. Having graduated Stanford, both first and second degree in finance and economics, he decided to dedicate his PhD to "Corruption and Petroleum in Developing Countries", following the recommendation of his tutor. A leading authority on matters of economics and home to some of the best experts in this field, the LSE is one of the world's best academic institutions. Many of the students come to earn a complete degree, whereas many other only come for short courses and specific certificates. The LSE has its fair share of students from Third World countries, with quite a few taking their rightful place at the top of their countries' economic leadership. While a student, McLeigh cultivated many ties with students from the

Third World. Nevertheless, the name Mngushe did not ring a bell.

- Set an appointment for next week, during the international gathering of central bank chiefs. One hour, mind you.

*

The following Tuesday, when Liz laid out his agenda for that particular day, McLeigh noticed that his appointment with Dr. Mngushe was set between the governor of the Bank of Singapore's address on "China's Impact on Capital Movements in Asia" the traditional lunch with the heads of several European central banks. At precisely twelve o'clock, Liz buzzed him to say Governor of the Central Bank of Jeronti, Dr. Mngushe, had arrived for their meeting. McLeigh recognized him as his longtime friend from the LSE, but also recalled that back then, Dr. Mngushe went by "Handsome John".

- So how am I to call you? 'Sir Bernard McLeigh' or 'Barry'?
- And am I supposed to call you? 'John', or 'His Excellency Central Bank Chancellor Dr. Mngushe'?

They were evidently glad to reunite, especially as the meeting would have afforded them the opportunity to reminisce from their bygone uni days. Nevertheless, "business before pleasure", all the more so as McLeigh remembered his guest was a Muslim, so 'pleasure' could not include a shot of fine whisky.

- How may I help you?
- My government is two or three billion dollars short.
- You require a loan? Some sort of backing?
- No, thank you.
- I don't follow, then. What are you asking for, in that case?

- My government was robbed to the tune of billions of US dollars and I have good reason to believe they are here in England.

- What makes you think so?

Sir Bernard heard him out and availed himself of the full scope of his guest's suspicions.

- Most fascinating. Riveting stuff. Give me a few days to look into it and see how I might be able to be of assistance. In the meantime, I will have Liz reserve us seats at a good restaurant. You are in for a treat, believe me. See you this evening.

*

- Hiya, Bob. Pull up a chair and pour yourself a cuppa. Me too. I have a fine tale for you.

The Bank of England's security chief, a tall and scrawny fella, filled up two fine china cups, per McLeigh's instructions. He sat himself down, ready for the fun that those meetings always proved to be. They were longtime friends, ever since his days as a senior figure at Scotland Yard, while the chancellor was in charge of the police budget while working at the treasury. Their friendship was long enough for him to know that whatever the talk was going to focus on, it will conclude, without fail, with a glass of some extra fine single malt whisky from the bottom left drawer of McLeigh's desk.

- Right before lunch, I had an interesting meeting with an old friend. He currently heads the Central Bank of Jeronti. He told me something that sounds straight out of those Agatha Christie paperbacks he used to love reading so much. This story has corruption, smuggling and disguise. The gist of it is that he believes we have billions of dollars belonging to Jeronti stashed right here in England. Had I not known him, and had I not been aware of Jeronti's importance to the UK, I would have sent him packing. Nevertheless, I decided to get to the bottom of it. As this is a matter of the utmost discretion, I thought it best to involve you.

- What is it that you want of me?

- Please clear up some of your special time and figure out how you might be able to help my friend.

A week barely went by, and Bob reported back to McLeigh.

- I put my inquiry concerning your friend's matter on the back burner. But not on your behalf, but rather thanks to what you're keeping in that bottom drawer.

Bob stretched his long legs and allowed himself to do something no else had ever done at no central bank chief's office. He raised his legs and laid his feet on the chair beside him.

- So, what would you like to know?

- Well, is the dosh there or not?

Bob was looking smug.

- I've got a good reason to keep to the point. You may tell your friend it's "no dice". No 'dosh' as you call it. The money isn't in England.

- Just as I thought. I'll have Liz put a call through to Jeronti now.

- Hang on. That kind of an answer would not have taken me a week. You gave me a hot potato, but I didn't let it go. According to my findings, both the government of Jeronti on the one hand and numerous businessmen from this country do have many bank accounts here in England. But these accounts are under scrutiny. They are constantly being monitored and controlled and are an integral part of the banks' financial reports. We are part of that oversight anyway. Consequently, no bank in the UK would dare keep on record any funds whose sources is so tall as those Agatha Christie tales your friend has a passion for.

- Liz, please get me the Governor of the Bank of Jeronti.

- I am not done yet. My inquiries did uncover something the governor of the Bank of England must look into at some point.

- I knew you'd pass the parcel back to me. What is it?

- I discovered we are home to a thriving industry of schemers, all sorts of people entrusted with the shady business of laundering funds for foreign nationals through a string of various front accounts at all sorts of tax havens.

- Is there an issue with violations against our laws? Shall I call Sir Gallgood?

- Never mind the legal counselor for now. Let's concern ourselves with your friend. According to my findings, the leading figure among these finance types is a London barrister. I checked the ports and airports and came across a record of his unaccountable comings and goings. This list has lent further credence to my already mounting suspicions: this attorney from London has been leaving the country very often, always going to the Cayman Islands, Panama City, the Channel Islands and other such romantic locations. If your friend would like to pursue those funds, then he would do well to see that attorney. Now, crack that bottle open.

A few seconds later, Liz had Dr. Mngushe on the line.

- If you would like your government's funds back, then you'd better have a chat with Attorney John Henry Byrot of number thirty-four Bailey Street. Please bear in mind though, you are on your own. We're not party to this. I am merely lending an old friend a hand.

- Thank you. Next time, dinner is my treat.

*

The headquarters of the Bank of England have for a long time been situated at this grand Victorian edifice in the City of London. The moment Byrot arrived to see the governor, Sir McLeigh left his office to greet him very cordially and led him in by the hand. Byrot was surprised to find three other guests waiting for him at McLeigh's office: an elegant man of African origin, who was presented to him as the governor of the bank of Jeronti, as well as two other black gentlemen in well-tailored suits that seem to have been hastily fitted, maybe even on the way to that very appointment. McLeigh presented them to Byrot but left out either their titles or positions.

- I realize this meeting must come as a surprise to you. Nevertheless, my old friend here, a close colleague from Jeronti, has asked me to set up this appointment. I am not one to turn a good friend down. At any rate, I gather this talk has nothing whatsoever with my position, so I leave you to it. You are welcome to avail yourselves of my office as I take my lunch.

Byrot was facing the three men all by himself now. He noticed the calm demeanor of the central bank chief, which was a stark contradiction to the stern looks the other two men gave him. The four men proceeded to exchange a few pleasantries. After which Dr. Mngushe turned to Byrot.

- My dear Mr. Byrot. It has taken us quite a while to look you up and realize the enormous assistance you can offer us. We are here in London on a national mission whose goal is to reimburse the people of Jeronti those ill-gotten gains stolen from them. We are sure that being the honest advocate and person that you are, you would not deny the men and women of Jeronti your kind assistance.

- What do you want of me? What would you have me do?

- We have a mutual acquaintance by the name of Biko. We have it on good authority that you are in close proximity to the high sums our mutual friend had stolen from the people.

- I have no clue what you're talking about, and even if I did, I am still at a loss as to what you could possibly want with me.

- We're not asking for much, merely that you deliver us the details of Biko's accounts.

- Without actually referring to what you've just said, you must be familiar with my adherence to attorney-client privilege. I am quite sure you've checked my background, so you must know that not only have I never betrayed a client, I have no wish to do so in the future either.

- We truly value you and your professional discretion. Fully aware that attorneys never work without some sort of pay, we are therefore prepared to leave you ten percent of any sum retrieved to us thanks to you.

Byrot was taken aback by this last statement from Dr. Mngushe, and said:

- Now look here, doctor, this isn't a question of money. It's a matter of principle.

One of the two gentlemen, who until now grappled with his tight-fitting tie, turned to Byrot.

- I'm afraid you've got it backwards. We haven't come here to negotiate with you. We are here to receive our funds back. You've got forty-eight hours to give us your answer.

Byrot felt his temper surging:

- I don't need forty-eight hours. I am on my way to lunch. Sir McLeigh's secretary will show you out.

He rose from his seat, leaving the other three guests stunned in their seats.

*

Two days after the meeting at McLeigh's office, Rosaline came into Byrot's chambers. He had told her he was planning to work through the weekend since he was due abroad again at the beginning of the following week. She returned to the office the following Monday at nine o'clock. That makes it six days after the meeting with the gentlemen from Jeronti.

The lights were on in Byrot's room, so Rosaline knocked on the door softly to say good morning but there was no reply. When she came in, she saw, much to her horror, Byrot in his armchair, his head resting on his desk. Rigor mortis had set in, as she could tell by the part of his face she could make out.

*

Scotland Yard showed up a short while later. A little after that, an urgent telex from Jeronti's embassy in London reached President's Imru's office in Golasa: "FYI: Attorney Byrot was found dead!"

*

The committee for retrieving the funds reconvened once again at the president's chief of staff. Mkume Shibu had on his usual colorful getup.

- Does anyone have anything to report?

Ominous silence descended on the room. Dr. Mngushe

volunteered to go first.

- I tried to track down the funds. For this purpose, I traveled to London and met with my friend, the chancellor of the Bank of England, Sir McLeigh. But I am not the bearer of good tidings. My inquiries revealed Biko did not keep the money in the UK.

- Where then?

- With the help of my English friend, I was able to find the key person for accessing the funds, but shortly after our meeting with him, six days in fact, he was found dead. There are strong suspicions he was murdered.

- What does that mean?

- That we haven't got a lead as to the money's whereabouts.

- Anyone care to add anything?

No one volunteered.

- Words cannot convey the depths of my disappointment. As far as I'm concerned, President Imru gave us an order. We can only follow and obey. Since neither of you were able to retrieve the money, I shall have to see to it on my own. Dismissed!

CHAPTER 12

'Twas an autumn day with a hint of winter. Assaf couldn't really tell, either because rain had set in early or because he was feeling light and idle that day. The phone yanked him out of his slumber.

- Hello, Mr. Shlomi. I hope I'm not disturbing you.
- Who is this?
- Mkume Shibu, chief of staff for the president of Jeronti. Surely you remember me. I was a student in the Mossad program a few years ago. I gave an address on graduation day. I did promise you our paths shall cross one of these days. Well, that day has come. We have an important and urgent matter, and we'd like you help. We found a British Airways flight that's leaving Tel Aviv for Jeronti via London tomorrow morning at eight o'clock. We book a seat for you and we await your arrival. Thus, seated in first class, Assaf Shlomi spent his flight from London to Jeronti wondering about this urgent invitation. His long career in the intelligence business taught him the answer will present itself, so he soon fell asleep until landing.

*

A black Mercedes pulled up right near the plane at Jeronti

airport. Two men in black trousers and white shirts got out of the car, went over to Assaf, and asked him to come into the car with them. An escort car followed suit, and so both cars stormed onto the main road connecting the airport to Golasa.

As much as Assaf was familiar with the road, he felt it was busier than during his last visit, especially going into town. Thousands of cars, crawling bumper to bumper and an untold number of motorized Kiki rickshaws filled the never ending traffic. The streets were teeming with people. So much so, he couldn't even see the sidewalk. At some point, the driver turned the siren and flashing lights on to make way through traffic, all the way to the Hilton downtown.

- I hope two hours should be enough for you to rest. We'll be waiting for you at the lobby and take you straight to the presidential palace when you come down.

If it were up to him, Assaf would not have minded a longer rest at the penthouse suite they had reserved for him, but his curiosity on the one hand and the tight schedule his hosts kept on the other, meant he was soon back in the same Mercedes. Upon arrival at the president's palace, Assaf was taken to see the chief of staff. Sure enough, Mkume Shibu, all dressed up in some multicolored getup, was indeed waiting for him. He hugged Assaf and kissed him, after which he took him to see the president at the latter's luxurious offices, where a huge copper fruit bowl stood upon this long mahogany table. Next to the many colorful fruits stood a crystal carafe filled with yellow pineapple wine. The host poured himself and his guest, then two additional men in the room, who wore western suits.

The customary toast was made, followed by the usual pleasantries. Shibu then excused himself and returned a few moments later, wearing a well-tailored suit that accentuated his height and broad shoulders.

- I am so please to see you, my old friend. You are a number one pro!

'*Why is he referring to me as an old friend?*'

- Thanks for the compliment, but what do you know about me?

- More than you give us credit for. We know more than you might think: for instance, we know who it was that nabbed that terrorist in Guinea, the one who killed two Israelis here in Jeronti. We also know who tipped off our intelligence services as to the terrorist squad that arrived under the auspices of the Iranian embassy. Don't take it personally, but we also know who set the Ibu tribes against one another, only to sell them lots of arms and then mediate peace. I could cite many more examples, but then we would have no time left to discuss the matter that has brought you here.

Assaf's face remained frozen.

- Allow me not to comment about all that. So what now? What's the point of this meeting?

- Our president decided finally to end the scourge of corruption in this country. He can at last make good on his promise to put a stop to the bribery and to the robbery of the people's coffers perpetrated by a small group of people that beset the country and distribute the national revenues equally between everyone.

- That all sounds very well, but what does it have to do with me?

- We know the lion share of the funds stolen, the proceeds of this corruption, is held out the country. The president has issued an order to retrieve this money.

- Can you please clarify?

- Certainly. Until a few months ago, before we came to power, one of the ministers in the former government was a man called Biko Bwana. We know he received billions of dollars in bribes during his term in office. He deposited those funds in banks worldwide. It was decided to take whatever means to have these funds returned to Jeronti.

- What have you done thus far about this Biko person?

- We discovered he had been living in England. We tried every way to contact him and convince him to give up the money. We were even willing to consider offering him immunity from prosecution, but he's refusing to hear from us. He wouldn't even agree to make indirect contact.

- Why haven't you approached the English? I know the British government is highly sensitive when illegal funds are involved.

- We certainly do not need you for this sort of advice. That hardly merits a first class ticket here.

- Thanks. Still, what did you do?

- We made use of all our contacts in the UK, all the way to the governor of the Bank of England. It turns out the funds we are looking for are not held there. Besides, British law enforcement authorities can do nothing in relation to those funds.

- So what have you done?

- We succeeded in getting to the person who had handled all those funds for Biko.

- Great! All's well that ends well!

- It's far more complicated than neutralizing that arms dealer in Sudan.

- Kindly allow me not to comment on any personal snide remarks. Who is this guy who handled the funds on behalf of your 'patient' and what have you done with him?

- His name is Byrot. An attorney by trade. We managed to get to him and did try to convince him to help us get the money back, but he wouldn't hear of it.

- You probably didn't offer him enough money.

- It's not a question of money. He offered up a few statements our people were unclear about: "fiduciary", "attorney-client privilege", "professional discretion" and the like, but before we could even ask for any clarification, we were out the door.

- I told you: you didn't offer him enough.

- Truth be told, we thought so too. We were about to make another appointment to see him, but then it all went wrong.

- What do you mean?

- I told you this affair was more complicated than getting those hostages in Somalia freed.

- You mean Sudan.

- Whatever. Turns out this Byrot person invested a large chunk of Biko's money in Panama City, where a front man of his opened up these bogus accounts, where millions of dollars were deposited, but when Byrot sensed something was fishy, he went over to Panama himself to tip the front man off, only to discover it was he who had been defrauded. They pulled quite a stunt on him.

- This is getting interesting. Then what?

- Byrot found out his own front man was a crook, that all the bank accounts were gone. They sure did a number-

- Whoa! This *is* more like Somalia than Sudan.

- Hang on, we're not done yet. Byrot decided to investigate the disappearance of all that money, even though he was told to leave the matter alone. Turns out a stubborn old timer like him just can't take a hint. A few hours before we were about to surprise him with another meeting, his secretary found him dead at his own desk in London.

- So what does that leave us with?

- That leaves us with Byrot, who was finished off, so we were told, by some South American mob gang, and with Biko, who cannot be persuaded in any way shape or form to return his ill-gotten gains peacefully.

- I am beginning to realize why you brought me over. Such a story does merit first class tickets.

- So to business, then. We are asking for your help in getting Biko to Jeronti.

- What will you do with Biko here in Jeronti?

- That's no concern of yours. I don't mind telling you we are confident that once he is here, the money will soon follow.

- I need a week to consider your offer.

- Fine, but no longer than that. The president is pressing the issue. First class roundtrip.

*

Assaf was back at Shibu's office one week later.

- I've looked into your proposal and I am willing to accept it, provided you agree to a few terms.

- Let's hear them.

- First of all, I am sure you know I am no longer in the service of my country. I am a private individual. Our agreement must not have any bearing on the State of Israel.

- Fine.

- Secondly, I shall head this operation and organize everything, but please be clear that I cannot be the front man. Every entry I make into the UK is monitored and recorded.

- Agreed.

- I shall draw up the plans for the operation. Exclusively. You will help me in any way you can, swiftly and efficiently.

- Done.

- I shall choose my own team and there will be an iron wall between my staff and your guys on the ground. Full compartmentalization.

- Of course.

- The budget is ten million dollars, to be deposited in a secret Swiss bank account only I will have any access to.

- Sure thing.

- I suggest we reconvene here tomorrow. I shall explain the kind of assistance I shall be requiring on your end, as well as my proposed timetable for the operation.

- See you tomorrow. I knew I could count on you.

*

- Well, as I've told you yesterday, I shall be assuming the entire operational part of Biko's abduction. You will see to the administrative side. For instance, make sure a cargo plane from your national airline lands at Stansted on a date I shall give you. This plane will carry a box, made per my specifications. We need this box to be boarded onto the cargo plane without being inspected. How it's done is your problem.

- Fine. We can address that: according to international conventions, diplomatic cargo is exempt from inspection. We shall see to it.

- Agreed then. I suggest we hold our next meeting, on coordination, in ten days' time. We shall also approve the operation's detailed plan. Good luck!

CHAPTER 13

The house on Tel Aviv's King George Street was built way back in the 1930s. Its old exterior imbued respectability, all the more so with the row of old sycamores at the center, their branches shading over the building's windows. Assaf climbed the old stairs, passed by two formerly green wooden doors on the first floor that fully conveyed the ravages of time, and reached the second floor. The apartment's front door had only recently been replaced: a wood-paneled metal door with a steel doorframe. Assaf spotted an eye inspecting him through the looking hole.

- Who is it?

- It's Assaf. Don't you recognize me anymore?

Two bolts swiveled and a surprised look greeted Assaf.

- How did you find me?

- I made my way to locations way more secret than this, some of which, as I recall, with you.

- But where have you disappeared to?

- Well, after my escapade in South Africa, I had to retire from the entire world for a while and take some time to myself. How about you, Assaf?

- I'm doing great. I retired from the service and went into private business for myself.

- What is that you do exactly?

- That's exactly what I wanted to discuss with you, but I have this rule: there are matters I do not discuss in people's apartments.

- Fine, so let's set up a meeting.

The café on Tel Aviv's Dubnov Street was Assaf's favorite spot: a mere five minute walk east of numerous government hubs and five minutes north of most of Tel Aviv's prime culture centers. In addition, the town's fine dining and various entertainment venues lay a short walk west and south of the café where one may find a conveniently located, friendly and not too expensive parking lot. All the fine things the big city has to offer. The coffee shop itself is a quiet, pleasant joint, boasting a spacious terrace shaded by tall ficus trees with leafy branches, which lend a cool, intimate atmosphere in the summer. Assaf's favorite perch here is the southwestern corner, a small enclave among the cobblestones sporting a round table with four chairs. Whenever he felt the need to relax and wanted some privacy, this is where he would come, commune with his double espresso and buttered croissant and find the perfect peace he sought. Assaf would sometime avail himself of this corner for the purpose of discrete rendezvous with a more welcoming atmosphere than dull offices or generic hotel lobbies. This is where he invited Eli over.

- You still haven't told me how you found me.

- To tell you the truth, it wasn't easy. It was simpler to track you down at that prison back in Johannesburg than in Tel Aviv.

- You're probably right. I waited night and day to see you in prison, or at the very least one of your people, but you never showed up.

- What have you been doing with yourself since they let you out?

- When I got back to Tel Aviv, I decided to isolate myself completely. Besides, as you know, I had to detach myself from everything per the terms of my release.

- Yes, I'm familiar with them. In fact, I took part in drawing them up. But your house arrest was over a year ago, and the restrictions on the State of Israel and its various agencies as far as you're concerned do not stop you from working in any line of work that's unrelated to the government.

- I know, but this self-imposed period of laying low suited me. It might be time to return to the living. How about you? I heard you retired from the service.

- Yes, I did. So, we're both retired, both prohibited from pursuing stuff that's connected to the government. Nevertheless, life is full of surprises.

- What do you mean? Something that might give me a rush of adrenaline?

- For sure. I'd like to pick your brain about something, and perhaps even bring you in on an operation, but I do feel the need to tell you that unless we reach an understanding, you must forget about everything we are about to discuss. Besides, why is a grown man like you ordering hot chocolate for, like some child?

- If all you did was lay rotting in some prison cell in J'burg, dreaming about a cup of hot chocolate the whole time, you wouldn't be asking that. So, what's this all about?

- I just got back from Jeronti. I've got a few admirers there.

- There too?

- Yeah. They made me an offer. It's quite interesting, in fact. I had enough time during my flight to arrive at the conclusion I would like you in on it with me.

- Why me of all people?

- Well, first off, it's not a one man show. Second, I cannot be the front man in all this. Thirdly, if I am going to cooperate with anyone, then the only person who comes to mind is someone who thinks one plus one equals three.

- Where did you hear that?

- That's what people say about you.

- And why can't you be the front man? You've suddenly become modest?

- I'll let you in on the whole story in a moment, but first, if I've got fans in Jeronti, I am sure to have my share of fans back in London as well, which isn't my cup of tea. Whenever I land in the UK, I always see the person at passport control reach under the table. Wherever I might be, I always receive a friendly call asking me how I'm doing.

- OK, I'm sold. So, what's this all about, then?

- One of the former ministers in Jeronti's previous government fled the country the moment the coup broke out, but not before laying his hands on a few billion dollars.

- That's hardly anything new.

- The new thing about this is that the new president, Imru, vowed to retrieve those funds, no matter what. When I asked them what they have done about it, they said, well, according to their version, they did whatever they could to get the money back legally. But they've failed, partly because when they tried to get the attorney involved in smuggling those funds and hiding them to assist them in reclaiming the money back, well, before they could convince him, he was found dead.

- Amateurs!

- No. They swore to me they had nothing to do with it.

- So what do they want from you?

- For starters, they want me to deliver a plan of action,

within a few days, mind you, to have the funds restored. They believe the only way is to have this minister brought back to Jeronti. They think that once he's back in the country, the funds will return as well.

- So what do you want from me?

- I already have an outline as to how to bring his excellency the former minister back to his native country. Nevertheless, as I've told you, this isn't an operation for just one person. This calls for a combined, sophisticated action - and you're the first person I thought of. I suggest you sleep on it. I'll see you tomorrow and we'll figure out how to take it from here. I know you well enough to be sure money is not your only motivation. Nevertheless, there's one million dollars US in it for you if it goes through without a hitch. That money might make life easier for you.

*

Couples in love tend to meet at the same intimate location. Assaf knew this rule does not apply to operational activities, so he told Eli to meet him at Cliff Beach. One of Assaf's favorite locations, this sandy beach stretches for miles between the splendid sea and the cliffs that are home to white, bell-shaped field bindweed and white sea daffodils.

As usual, Assaf arrived half an hour early. He placed his clothes on an orange table right in front of the waves and took a short walk in his shorts, his feet basking in the warmth of the sand and the cool waters in equal measure. When he got back from his walk, he spotted Eli waving to him from afar and waved back. They sat by the orange table. It was early morning, so there was no one else around.

- How do you come up with these locations?

- Don't tell me you've never heard of this place. Whenever I want to find some peace of mind or go someplace that can't be wiretapped or anything like that, this is where I go.

- Had I known such places existed when I was serving my time back in Johannesburg, I would have dreamed about it for sure, in addition to hot chocolate and Galia.

- If you like, you can tell me all about Galia sometime. But in the meantime, let's see how we're getting on from here.

- Look, Assaf, I did give it my serious consideration, and truth be told, your proposal does come at an opportune time. Ever since I was released, it appealed to me to be a shut in, a recluse. Even the guys from my old outfit in the service, who always wanted to come up and see me, I always told them no. It got to the point that even Galia began asking all sorts of questions, got up to all kinds of funny ideas. Your offer to bring me in on the action shook me. It made me decided to return to the stuff I am so familiar with, to go back to the way I was. I am on board, but only on two conditions: first, that at no point will there be any bloodshed; second, that whoever you bring in will also need to be absolutely fine by me as well.

- I find both your terms completely acceptable.

For the following three hours, the barefoot young waitress served them carrot juice, iced coffee and assorted sandwiches. When they concluded their plan of action and were done formulating it, they arranged to meet the following day in order to discuss who to bring in as the other team members.

*

It was Eli who decided where the next meeting would take

place. Assaf and Eli arrived at the Mikveh-Israel Botanical Garden at the appointed hour.

- I didn't want to ask you about it yesterday, but how the h*ll did you come up with this spot? What went through that mind of yours?

- First off, last time I was here, it was a school trip in eighth grade. I always knew I'd be back. Besides, you did say 'some place without any wire taps and the like,' so I figured this might serve us well in this regard; third: I was looking for a place that would blow you away.

They sat on a bench under this old gazebo, near a Washingtonia palm tree that's probably a hundred years old, or more. Once they were done with the details of the operation, they went back to the issue of assigning the roles.

- So we agreed upon a team of three. Any suggestions as to the other two members beside yourself?

- The doctor has a major role to play. This has to be an experienced and resourceful anesthesiologist, someone who can keep his wits about him. But the third man is the one who's the most important.

- I agree. I accept your position that you're not cut out to head the operation. It's best you do not hang around there before we take action. I also agree we need someone with the proper background to be in charge. Have you got anyone in mind?

- I know this anesthesiologist who works at a hospital. He's considered a first rate professional. We used him in various operations, and he always cooperated fully.

- What makes you think he'll go along? He'd be jeopardizing his license.

- I made a few calls prior to our meeting today. I discovered this doctor is in financial trouble. He sure could use the money. He wouldn't miss the opportunity to score a million dollars.

- Gotcha. How about the third man?

- It kept me thinking the entire night. I don't know whether his name will ring any bells, but I can tell you this much: if he says yes, and I have a pretty good reason to think he will, then we've found our guy.

- Does he need the money too?

- Not in the least. He wouldn't mind the million-dollar pay, but if he takes the job, it won't be because of the money.

- What then? Did you charm him into it?

- Dudi isn't the sort of person who could be fooled, certainly not by me. There, I've revealed his name to you, and you didn't recognize it.

- What makes you think he'll come on board?

- Because he's the sort of man who would never miss the chance of a good adventure.

- I am intrigued. Who is he?

- OK, here goes: Dudi and I go way back, to the beach in Netanya. He was born on the south side, the other side of the tracks, you might say, in a neighborhood renowned for its string of mobsters. I was born in a small rural suburb, into what they call 'a nice family', 'salt of the earth'. The beach brought us together and made us bond. We'd both skip school to go to the beach. At first, there was tension, but very early on, we got to know each other and became firm friends. He led this group of kids from his neighborhood and I had my own band of followers from where I grew up. Both teams used to meet and do all those things teenagers get up to. Truth be told, I idolized him. He's courageous, staunch, a born leader and gifted decision maker. We kinda began losing touch when I went to military boarding school and stopped being in each other's lives when I joined a combat unit and he didn't. His military service wasn't something to be proud of. Then, I heard rumors he became the head of some major criminal organization. I also heard they indicted him for murder about two years ago, that he did time for about a year and a half, but then they had to acquit him and completely exonerate him.

- So what made you suddenly think of him?

- The truth is I didn't suddenly think of him, because I never stopped thinking about him. I've never forgotten him. All during my time in the service, I kept thinking what a loss, that he could have made an extraordinary operative in the service of our country. The authorities made a mistake not recruiting him to a combat role and so on. All these years, I kept feeling jealous of him, thinking about the amazing life a guy like that must lead, without any boundaries, no rules, him being the only one calling the shots.

- You're getting sentimental!

- OK, so I won't go overboard. I'll just say that it's only a matter of chance, maybe luck, that each of us has led the kind of life we ultimately ended up with. It could have been the other way around just as easily.

- Meaning?

- It sometimes occurs to me that I have the makings of a criminal myself, whereas he could have been a top-notch Mossad operations chief.

- Have you nothing but good things to say about him?

- Certainly not. He's a very capable guy, he fits the bill to a tee, but you have to bear in mind we're talking about a tough guy, as tough as they come. He's stubborn, he's got no scruples and he doesn't flinch.

- I'm already curious to meet him.

- No problem. I'll set it up. I'll introduce you to him and offer him the lead role in this operation.

- Okay. Are we done here?

You can't leave without seeing the plot with the Cedars of Lebanon. See that big one over there by the corner? They say it was brought over from Lebanon a mere seedling, together with beams and the boards they used to build the First Temple. I know the Mossad doesn't put much stock in legends, but that sure is an impressive tree.

CHAPTER 14

- Hey Dudi, long time no see!

- Right. You disappeared into that obscure world of yours. I heard you retired.

- I take it you're in your own world of shadows, and never retired.

- Jealous? Wanna switch places again?

- No thanks, I would like to do something I've always dreamed about.

- What do you mean?

- Do something together.

- Sounds great. So? What are we talking about?

- So typical of you, always straight to the point. So, here's the deal: I've been approached by the leader of this African country. He and I have a mutual acquaintance. He told me about a former minister in the previous government of that country, who had stolen billions and hid them abroad. All diplomatic attempts to retrieve these funds have failed. I met with this African head of state and he told me flat out he believes I was the only person who could get the former minister to go back to that country.

- How are you supposed to bring him back?

- That's why I'm sitting here with you. He has asked me

to give him my reply within a few days. He also agreed to a substantial payment in exchange.

- What kind of operation are you talking about?

- An extraction. We'll kidnap this minister and deliver him to Africa.

- Wow, sounds like a scene right out of James Bond. I can see those movies we used to sneak into back in the day got to you.

- It's simpler than you think. I've already got a plan.

- Let's hear.

- The operation has two parts. The first phase is the actual action and the second is the administrative envelope.

- What does that mean?

- I reached an agreement with the government of Jeronti, according to which they will place a special cargo plane at our disposal, which we will use to transport the abductee to Jeronti. I will see to it that a special box is made and fitted onto the plane, which we will board, along with the minister inside that box.

- Who's going to be in charge of what?

- As much I would like to be part of the extraction team, I really think that's a bad idea. I am well known in the UK, and the operation requires a great deal of preparation. The moment the English find out I'm hanging around, they'll put a tail on me. Besides, I think you'll be better at it than me.

- You know the English authorities better than I do. What makes you think they'll let you get a box with a bunch of people on board a plane, just like that, unchecked, no questions asked?

- I took care of that as well. Per my agreement with the people from Jeronti, their security officer will come to the airport, stamp the box with a "diplomatic" emblem, rendering exempt from passport control. They do not inspect diplomatic pouches or anything designated as such.

- I don't like this plan.

- You don't trust me?

- I have this rule in life: "never trust anyone!"

- But I'm not just anyone. You know me better than I know myself. Besides, I am a pro. I have never failed.

- So what happened on that operation in Isfahan?

That was the very first time Dudi had ever seen Assaf "losing it". The color drained from his face. His eyes turned red and his hand reached out to hold on to something.

- How would *you* know about Isfahan?

- I told you, on more than one occasion: Dudi knows everything!

- But only four people knew about this operation! The prime minister, the minister of defense, the head of Mossad, and myself.

- And so did Dudi.

- I'm amazed! Had I still been there, I would order the General Security Service to have you arrested and interrogated to learn how you came by this information. Believe me, you're so lucky.

- You'd have me arrested? I would never do something like to you. At most, I might have you killed.

- Lucky for us, then, that I don't have to arrest you and you do not have to kill me. We'd both pull it off.

- Let's go back to this "administrative envelope" business. What do you know about Jeronti's national airline?

- It's a pretty good company. They use pilots trained in the UK. They've got a good reputation. In our case, the cargo plane will be flown by veteran pilots who will be waiting for us at Stansted Airport, at a prearranged spot.

- What do they know about the operation?

- Not a thing. Neither the pilots nor the airline have an inkling as to the purpose of the flight. They think it's about transporting some sort of special, important, defense equipment. Their role amounts to landing the plane and then returning it back to Jeronti, without them actually knowing anything about the cargo.

- But we're still dependent upon them.

- Yes, that's true, but that would have been just the same with any other airline. Believe me, I would have preferred El Al just like you would, but do not forget, this isn't 1960 and we're not smuggling Eichmann from Argentina to Israel.

- Let's move on, then. I do not care for this business with the box. If we have it made in the UK, that's only asking for trouble.

- What do you mean?

- It's not your run of the mill kind of project. The contractor might be obliged to report any unusual order to the authorities. We have to take into account the possibility that someone may plant reconnaissance devices, tracking and so on, inside the box. Another thing to remember is that we must have some special kind of life support system inside the box in order to make sure that whomever is inside makes it to Jeronti alive.

- So what are you suggesting?

- The box has to be constructed someplace completely safe, far away from the UK and under our supervision. The anesthesiologist ought to provide his specifications for the box to make sure the 'client' stays alive.

- Roger that. I'll handle this issue vis-à-vis the authorities back in Jeronti and make sure all the points you've raised are addressed. What else?

- The last bit is the one I am troubled by the most: getting him on board the plane. It's a matter of only three minutes, but it can fk up the entire operation.

- There are serious people behind this thing. They're addressing the problem you highlighted head on. They also have a great man at the embassy, a graduate of the Mossad training school. He'll be handling the actual loading of the box on board in person.

- Still, he is a stranger. I'd like to meet him to get a sense of what he's like.

- I just knew you'd ask that, but sorry, no go. This is a very sensitive operation as far as the government of Jeronti is concerned, so they are unwilling to let even more people know about it. The circle must be kept tight and small.

- Don't you trust me?

- Of course I do, but that's not the issue. Since it matters this much to you, I'll try to get their consent again for one of you to meet the military attaché.

- If you want me to head the operation, that's a must. When I make a commitment to someone, I deliver. But when it comes to this operation, I am dependent on external factors I have no control over, one of whom is the glorified former head of Mossad operations' wing. And you ask me '*in amazement*' how I know about Isfahan...

- Don't bring this up again! I promise you I shall find out what you have to do with that particular operation and how you learned about it. In the meantime, let's move on. This thing is right up our alley. Besides, there's quite a windfall in it for us.

- The thing is, if anything goes wrong, you'll be sitting in some command post in Tel Aviv or Switzerland, whereas I will have to do time, which is the best-case scenario.

- I assume full responsibility for the administrative envelope. I'll have you know I do not normally take such a commitment upon myself.

- You are in it big time. That's quite a commitment. You know I can collect if need be. Another issue I would like to raise is the vehicle we'll be using for the hijack.

- Don't you worry, I haven't forgotten.

- What is it?

- We have a skilled driver who knows London like the back of his hand, better than any cabby. The Jeronti side will hire the proper car and will make sure no one will be able to put the driver and the vehicle together. They will erase any link between the two. The driver is supposed to return the car back to the company and leave the UK for the coming twenty-five years.

- How did you find the driver?

- He isn't English. He has been working for Jeronti's embassy in London for many years. Perfect record. His loyalty is beyond reproach. His lips are sealed.

- I insist on meeting him in person. I need to get a first-hand impression of his personality, of his ability to handle pressure, how he would be able to plan the actual drive and the escape route.

- Not a problem. I'll make a note of it and add it to the list.

- The doctor as well. He should be able to tell us what his requirements are in relation to the car. I attach very high importance to the doctor's involvement in the operation. Don't forget: we need to deliver this person alive, in one piece.

- I completely agree. Let's call it a day and meet back in two weeks' time to make sure all the details are ironed out. We'll set up a timetable and green-light the operation.

- To tell you the truth, I can hardly wait.

- Me too. I've been dying to get things started from the moment they approached me with this operation.

*

- So, what have we got?

- I did not waste my time. I've been to Jeronti. They'll have the box made. The team in charge is this crew of carpenters that are normally assigned to the presidential palace. They will build it per our specifications, complete with the anesthesiologist's demands. The material will be natural wood, the kind that 'breathes', to make it easier on whomever is inside. The box will also have upper vents and vents at its floor as well. The floor itself will be padded and the box will have its own electric outlet for lighting and the requirements of our crew's equipment. The box will also have a comfy bed, with straps or some other means of restraining our 'client'.

We have yet to resolve the issue of the toilet. Once we take off, it will be possible to open the box door and use the cockpit's WC.

- Oh? Okay.

- The actual construction of the box will be divided between one team that builds it, and another crew, which will install the infrastructure. We'll place an order for the bed with a third team and will ultimately attach the bed to the box on board the cargo plane itself. All the specifications of the box, getting on board and attaching it to the aircraft's floor have been personally coordinated with the operations chief of Jeronti's national airline company. He was the one who chose the pilots and he assumes personal responsibility for their performance, skills and character.

- That sounds much better than the previous idea, to have the box made in London, but something's still troubling me.

- What's on your mind?

- All this business with the box, how many people are involved?

- We made sure the whole chain does not exceed ten individuals in total, who are connected. In fact, there's no interaction between any of them: the carpenters do not know the pilots, who in turn are not familiar with the upholsterers. Not one of these people has a clue as to what the operation is. The pilots, who are the closest to the field, know the purpose of the whole thing is to transport some sort of highly sensitive defense equipment. They know they are not allowed to leave the aircraft at any point while on layover in London.

- Is that so?

- Bear in mind, also, that all these works are being carried out back in Jeronti, and if they reach the conclusion the project needs to be discrete, they know how to conceal it.

- Good.

- As for the extraction car, it's done. When you go to London next week, set up a meeting with the driver and coordinate everything you want with him. He is expecting your call. My role in all this is to give you his phone number. The rest is on you. The military attaché and the driver are working on the route. The driver will report on everything when you see him.

- Oh, Okay.

- We'll meet up again after you get back from London. We'll use this meeting to finally approve the plan and determine the zero hour. Enjoy London. Don't forget to have a beer for me at Sweeny Bar. They serve good beer there. And another thing: I know you're not in it for the money. Nevertheless, we have to discuss it too: your share of the operation stands at one million dollars.

- Not too bad for a couple of day's work.

*

- Do you know Eli Alon? No, of course you don't. I know him from my line of work, the 'world of shadows'. Few people know him, but those who do, know he's an exceptional, original, bold and creative man. There's no like him. I've already spoken to him about the proposal from Jeronti in general and he sounded keen. Together, we can make a fabulous team. A dream team. What do you say?

- Shlomi, do you remember our chats at the beach in Netanya before those arrests, and after? I told you back then all I was looking for was the thrill of it, life outside boundaries. I haven't changed, and I have no intention of changing. Unlike you, though, I never retired, quite the opposite, in fact. I have business all over the world and so many people have an axe to grind. Whatever I do, I examine it very carefully. I want your word, which you know how much I respect, that this guy who's supposed to join us, Eli, is an upstanding man, credible. That I'm not setting myself up for some trap here.

- You have my word.

- So where and when are we gonna meet?

*

The girls at the beach in Netanya the following day could not look away: the sight of three men in skimpy bathing suits walking up and down the beach was not something they could just pass by. One man was tall and only slightly overweight, but he was wearing this ridiculous cap. The other was blond and breathtakingly buff with deep blue eyes, and the third was brown, tall and sporting an impressive six-pack. Much to the girls' disappointed, the three men borrowed three plastic chairs from the lifeguard's station, took them way deep into the strip of sand and sat themselves far from any prying ears or watchful gazes.

- So it's settled, then. Assaf will speak with the doctor, after which he will go over to Africa for final coordination with our friends there.

CHAPTER 15

One day Dima finished an ordinary routine surgery and left the operating room to wash his hands and take off his scrubs.

"You have a visitor. He's been waiting for you for two hours now. I did tell him you were in the middle of an operation, but he preferred to wait for you," the ward's secretary told him as he was leaving.

Dima wasn't accustomed to any visitors, least of all at the hospital. Puzzled, he went to the end of the corridor, where this tall, fair-haired man with strong features and piercing blue eyes was sitting. This man rose to greet him, shook Dima's hand and said:

- I know you. You're Dr. Dmitry Blog. My name is Assaf Shlomi, is there some quiet place where we can speak?

Dima's surprise guest was the quintessential silent type. Strong with a firm handshake, but most of all, Dima was impressed by the fact that his visitor knew him, although they had never met. For a moment, it occurred to him that those former 'comrades' of his from Moscow may have finally caught up with him to have that 'talk' he had been dreading for so long. But something about this guy's demeanor made Dima dismiss any possible connection between the visitor and those operatives. At his request, the secretary directed them to one of the doctors' rooms, which happened to be vacant at that particular moment.

- How may I help you? How is it that *you* know *me*?

The guy looked directly into Dima's eyes.

- It doesn't matter where I know *you* from. I am here to help you.

- How could you help me? I don't remember asking for anyone's help.

- I have a proposal for you, a once in a lifetime offer: I am offering you one week's work for which you shall receive one million dollars.

Dima was taken aback. His visitor continued, not even allowing him time to react, neither to smile about it nor to cry over it.

- I will be calling you tomorrow. If you wish to hear the rest of the proposal, let's arrange to meet asap and finalize the details.

Since his arrival in Israel, Dima had been living in his tiny apartment rental near the hospital. The rent was low, as were his other living expenses. He saved most of what he earned each month for the days to come. Waiting for his wife and daughter, Dima had to contend with short phone calls every now and then, during which his wife Paulina would always tell him about her own work and how much she misses him. She would proceed to tell him that every night, when she's overcome by longing, she takes out the Uzbek jewel, which she never wore, holds it in her hand, and warms it, swearing her Dima would be the first person to put in on her neck.

On Saturdays, Dima took to taking his raggedy fourth-hand car on short drives to the small rural suburbs not far from where he lived, looking wistfully at the whitewashed houses with red roofs amid flower beds and grassy patches. 'I have a right dream too,' he told himself. '*One million dollars!*'

*

The meeting with Assaf Shlomi was set for Tuesday at half past two. Dima decided to take the whole day off, arrive in Tel Aviv early and stroll along the city's boardwalk, his favorite spot - his preferred location to think clearly, meditate and miss his family. Walking along the promenade, he wondered whether it was G-d who gave Paulina the color of her eyes, in honor of the sea, which was the inspiration, or whether the Almighty gave the sea its color, on that blessed day back at the time of creation, inspired by Paulina's eyes. '*Such nonsense. I miss her. I love her so much*'. He then broke off from the beach and went to some big shopping mall teeming with passers-by, large families, giggling girls, meanderers and people with real concerns. '*Everyone's in such a hurry*'. Despite the crowds and the little room to move along the passage ways, the stores themselves were pretty empty. Dima sat by this remote corner table at the food court, as instructed in advance. He faced the crowd and waited. He never stopped wondering about this baffling meeting and its purpose since that moment he saw Assaf at the hospital. The phone call he had received the previous day, announcing the meeting's time and place, increased his tension. This sum Assaf threw at him, one million dollars, sounded both terrifying and out of this world, immediately raising images of an oligarch from 'over there' and 'tycoons' from these parts. '*What do I, known as merely Dr, Blog, have to do with that kind of money? All I know is how to put people under... What would it take someone to do in order to deserve one million dollars? The whole thing's probably some joke, or some trap my former 'friends' have in store for me. Those people never give up on settling old scores. That said, perhaps there might be something in it after all? He did seem honest, he imbued credibility. I'd better hear him out,'* Dima concluded to himself.

The guy sat right in front of him exactly at the appointed hour, the epitome of calm and pleasant demeanor, stretching out his hand to greet him.

- I am Assaf, just in case you've forgotten. Yes, that guy from the hospital, the one who set up today's meeting.

Assaf was leaning forward, but this did not make him seem any less tall. His square jaw and his entire outward appearance spoke of strength and determination. His blue eyes focused on Dima.

- How is Paulina?

- Fine.

Dima answered automatically, only realizing how strange the question was after he replied. Once he regained his senses, he turned to Assaf, still puzzled.

- How do you know about Paulina?

- I initiated this meeting to talk business.

'Assaf did reply, but he ignored my question'.

- I require someone with your expertise in order to follow through on a project I'm working on. Just to keep you in the loop, seeing as there's no need to keep you in suspense, it's an operation whose purpose is the transfer of a person from a certain county in Europe to another country, in Africa.

- But who are *you*? How did you find me?

- I gave you my real name. Nevertheless, whereas you know nothing about me aside from that, which is a great deal, I do know a lot about you, from your fk up back in Moscow, through your flight number from Moscow to Vienna, to those small services you provide certain friends here in Israel from time to time. I hope that's enough for you. Just in case it isn't, I can tell you your shoe size.

Dima was stunned. He wanted to ask Assaf again how he had come by Paulina's name, but the possible answer scared him, so he kept quiet.

Assaf read Dima's mind.

- You have a lovely wife. We wouldn't be sitting here today unless we were sure about that.

He then turned to the waitress:

- I'd like two coffees, please, one strudel for this gentleman and a butter croissant for me, provided it's fresh!

The waitress took the order. Dima felt queasy. 'How does this strange man know about my addiction to strudels?' Nevertheless, he quickly replied.

- So, are you proposing I get involved in something illegal?

- That depends how you look at it. The people I'm organizing this operation for believe this course of action is the most humane, so much so that the people who would be carrying it out should get a medal from United Nations Human Rights Council.

- But you're proposing an act of violence?

- Not in the least! If that were the case, we wouldn't need your services as an anesthesiologist, would we? We'd be going it alone. Your role is to deliver the 'client' safe and sound, completely intact.

- What do I have to do exactly?

- Administer the sedatives, keep the guy unconscious for the duration of the journey and bring him back in one piece.

I would like to reiterate this operation is sanctioned by a legitimate government. An entire country is behind it.

- Assuming I agree, what am I supposed to do?

- We need your official consent within forty-eight hours, after which the whole team will get together and go over the details. Here's a phone number. It's viable for one call, after which it will no longer be connected, so don't get it wrong. Besides, I haven't forgotten about the million dollars, so once you agree, we finalize that issue as well.

Assaf disappeared just as abruptly as he'd showed up. Dima remained fixed to his seat, staring at the streaming crowd hanging out at the mall. He did not require forty-eight hours to make his mind up. He called the burner phone and approved the follow-up meeting.

- Be there Thursday at two o'clock.

- Where?

- At your favorite spot.

Assaf then cut off. Dima called the number again, just to make sure this wasn't all a dream, only to hear the automatic message telling him the number he called was no longer in service.

*

He sat on the bench overlooking the Mediterranean on the Tel Aviv promenade on Thursday at one pm. He immersed himself in the blue landscape before him.

Assaf turned to Dima at exactly two o'clock:

- I'm so glad you decided to come on board. I'll have someone pick you up from home on Sunday at six pm.

- How did you know I'd say yes?

- You wouldn't have called otherwise, certainly not twice.

Assaf disappeared again.

'*How does he know where I live?*' Dima wondered, but he did not dare ask, fearing the obvious reply.

The following Sunday, at six sharp, a dark station wagon pulled up next to Dima's decrepit apartment building. He was already waiting at the entrance, having come down from his apartment on the third floor. When he recognized Assaf at the wheel, he went over, opened the front door on the right and took his seat next to him.

They drove off, heading out of town. Assaf seemed to be taking them north. They turned right toward this small farming community Dima had never been to. They crossed through this place and stopped near this old house at the end of the road. It seemed very much like the other houses there, surrounded by an orchard and sporting a slightly dilapidated looking patch of grass. Assaf parked the car in a small driveway between two large avocado trees. The house looked dark, save for a flash of light at the back.

Assaf and Dima walked in, crossed through the kitchen that seemed like no one had used for quite a while and entered the living room, where Dima saw, sitting in the corner, an elegant, well-groomed handsome man. This man was wearing a crisp white top, black trousers with a stripe all the way down and black shoes. He recognized the expensive brand and noted the guy's appearance only made the entire place look even shabbier.

- This is Dudi.

Dima felt Dudi's face was familiar somehow, but he couldn't for the life of him remember from where.

- You don't need to introduce me to Dima. He'll figure it out by himself in no time.

Dima then recalled how frantic the staff at the operating room was just the week before: a young man with shot wounds had been rushed into surgery -. A large group of cops appeared moments after the young man's arrival. They sealed the whole place off and prevented anyone from entering the operating room. Anxious, the nurses quickly updated the doctors that the young man being operated on is none other than the son of an infamous mobster. The corridor was teeming with numerous men that the police was busy detaining. Some of these men were tall and burly, obviously the mafia boss's men. They accompanied a group of crying women. Despite all this commotion, Dima could not take his eyes off this handsome man who was standing at the center of the crowd, exuding calm and confidence. Moreover, the man was exceptionally elegant in his shiny black shoes, crisp white shirt and black trousers with stripes on either leg.

The operation lasted several hours. Once the bullets were removed, the patient was taken to the recovery room, much to Dima's relief. The whole thing took him back to that botched operation in Moscow that changed his life so much.

- I can see you've remembered. My son got out of the hospital yesterday. He's doing fine. I went over there personally to thank the manager for the good treatment you all gave him.

- Yes, I know. The manager also told the staff you gave the hospital a donation. Half a million dollars. US dollars!

- Yes. I'd give my life for my Sephi.

The other person present in the living room then presented himself:

- My name is Eli Alon.

He was tall yet slightly slouching. He had on a pair of jeans and red sneakers. His face imbued strength and determination. *'This is a unique team of extraordinary men,'* Dima thought to himself as the meeting began.

Assaf turned to everyone and said:

- I'm due to fly to Jeronti in three days' time. I'll be finalizing the logistic details of the plan as well as the other aspects of the entire operation. I received the minister's address in London, so I suggest Dudi and Eli go to London to prepare the field work and tie up all the loose ends concerning the extraction car. I received assurances that the driver is an experienced man who will know how to deliver the *'goods'* to the airport in the shortest and safest way possible. The military attaché and the driver planned both the drive and the escape route. Nevertheless, I think you'd better meet the driver in person and perform a dry run of the escape route. You'll receive the driver's contact information by the time you fly out.

Assaf paused and then added the following:

- I've got additional news for you. I was cleared to have you both meet the attaché in person prior to the operation. I understand that you've arranged for Eli to meet him and that Dudi will meet with the driver. Good luck to you both. Does anyone have any questions? Yes, Dudi?

- I would like to finalize the doctor's role right now.

- What's wrong?

- There's nothing wrong, only that we took it upon ourselves to bring the *'goods'* back to Jeronti safe and sound. This is the doctor's responsibility, so I need to know if he's got a detailed timetable and a structured anesthesia protocol in place.

Assaf quickly responded:

- Yes, we do. According to the timetable I've prepared, I estimate the timeframe between the extraction and your arrival at Stansted Airport at about two hours. I've taken the traffic into account. Your layover at the airport, which we are about to discuss now, should not last more than two hours. The flight from London to Jeronti takes roughly seven hours, so our 'client' should be sedated for about eleven hours. Is that a problem, doctor?

- No, provided our 'client', as you refer to him, is healthy in general. Do we have his medical file? If we do not, then we'd better get it soon. Just so you know, such a protracted period of sedation usually involves another anesthesiologist, three experienced nurses and auxiliary staff, not to mention proper facilities and equipment. This is why the medical file is so crucial, so that we do not have any surprises. Now, what can you tell me about the box?

- We had a problem with the issue of loading cargo to the aircraft without customs inspecting its contents. Mossad has some experience with this sort of thing, the most famous case is of course the Eichmann operation, when he was taken from Argentina to Israel. But we won't be able to pull that off in the UK.

- So what do we do with the box?

- The solution was actually suggested by the Jeronti. They're supposed to send a special cargo plane to Stansted. This aircraft will be fitted with a box that will be taken off and placed on the runway after landing. The 'client' and doctor will get in. maybe Eli needs to get in there too, in order to make sure they are both safe. Dudi will have to clear off the moment they're in and get his ass back to Israel. As soon as they are in the box, a man from Jeronti's embassy will place a seal marking the box as "diplomatic mail", rendering it exempt from inspection when they bring it on board the plane, which will then take off and fly right back to Jeronti. Any comments, doctor?

- All this sounds very romantic. But what if he should wake up? What am I supposed to do with him then?

- First of all, you're supposed to make sure he does not come to. Second, the box can be opened from inside. In either case, we'll open its door the moment after we take off.

- We have to make sure the box has a bed with safety belts to keep him from falling during the flight. I shall see to the sedation kit, but you have to provide me with emergency resuscitation, the plane must be equipped with it. Please see to it, just in case.

- Anything else?

- Yes. The 'extraction vehicle' as you call it has to be wide enough to lay this person flat on his back, along with enough room for me to be beside him and monitor him closely.

- Good luck to us all!

CHAPTER 16

'It's the same wine and the same assortment of fruit as before, but not quite the same,' Assaf thought to himself. The carafe of pineapple wine, surrounded by crystal glasses, indeed stood at the exact location as Assaf remembered from the previous meeting, but the produce gave off such a strong fresh scent it had to have been laid out only a few hours earlier.

Mkume Shibu and two of his senior advisors were already sitting around the table, paying close attention to Assaf.

- I return to you with a plan, but it hinges on two conditions: one - that it's going to be a clean operation without any bloodshed; second - that it will have nothing whatsoever to do with Israel, either directly or indirectly.

- Done. We accept both terms. What next?

- The plan we've formulated is to extract the minister in London and deliver him safe and sound to Jeronti. The plan is based on a clear separation of powers and duties between us and you. Our team will be in charge of abducting the minister and getting him to Stansted Airport. You will be in charge of the logistics as well as of the cooperation concerning the following issues: one, we need to receive your intelligence file on Biko, complete with the house where he resides, his security measures, the neighbors in the immediate vicinity, his contacts in London as well as any other helpful information; two, we need to have his medical chart, all his relevant medical data, including any ailments, what medications is he sensitive to, his blood pressure, his weight and any other relevant detail; three, a cargo plane waiting on the runway at Stansted at the appointed hour, in accordance with our prearranged timetable; four, the aircraft must be in prime operational condition, piloted by two senior pilots who must be discrete and trustworthy; five, the aircraft must be fitted to make a round trip from Jeronti to London and back; six, you'll fit the plane with equipment and facilities in accordance with the specifications we provide you; seven, you'll manufacture the box and the bed Biko is to be placed in, per the specifications we provide you; eight, you'll be responsible for bringing the box on board the plane; nine, you shall be tasked with getting the car ready, a vehicle suitable for the purpose of nabbing our '*client*', as well as a highly capable driver who can be trusted one thousand percent; ten, you shall appoint a contact person, a point-man, if you will, with whom I shall keep continuous contact. Now, if you agree to all this, we may proceed. Ah, and there's also the matter of the expenses.

- Thank you, Assaf. I knew we could count on you.

Shibu then continued.

- The president is pressing for an immediate resolution of this issue, so I'll make sure they bring you back to the Hilton now, and we'll meet here tomorrow morning, by which time you'll receive our replies to all your requests.

Assaf's enjoyed his sound sleep. He never had any trouble sleeping and would always pity his colleagues and friends who showed up to meetings looking like they hadn't had a good night's sleep. Whenever they would complain about a lack of shut-eye, he would mock them. The burden of thoughts and worries only served to make his sleep even heavier and sweeter.

He enjoyed his nice morning bath and a rich breakfast and came down to the lobby. A chauffeur in uniform picked him up from the entrance and drove him back to Shibu's extravagant offices.

Shibu greeted Assaf with a beaming smile. His aides were sitting on either side.

- I hope you slept well. You've asked us to appoint a liaison to streamline the operation. I would like to present the contact person.

Shibu himself rose from his seat and shook Assaf's hand warmly.

- It is I.

In response to Assaf's surprised look, Shibu quickly added:

- This only goes to show you how crucial this matter is, as far as President Imru is concerned. He attaches such high importance to the operation, that he had me take a two month leave of absence from everything else in order to dedicate my entire time to promoting this endeavor. Besides, it gives me great pleasure to be working with you and your brave men. As for the logistics, we have accepted all your requests.

Shibu proceeded to list them: "One, for the purpose of this operation, we shall provide a cargo plane belonging to our national airline and flown by our best pilots; two, the plane will contain a box built per your specifications; three, the president personally instructed the security officer of our embassy in London to acquiesce to all your demands without exception; four, this security officer is responsible for getting the box on board the aircraft; five, he'll also provide you with any logistic assistance you require in London, including, for instance, a car and a driver, both suitable for the purpose of extracting Biko; six, the security officer will provide you our intelligence file on Biko; seven, as for the medical file, we need a few days as we haven't received all the material yet. As I've told you, I am at your service at any time. I hope to iron the remaining details out in the coming days. Now, as for the financial remuneration, the president set aside ten million dollars for this project. I hope you appreciate his generosity. He, in turn, hopes this investment will show a return, and its fruits be restored to the people. This sum covers any and all the expenses accrued in the framework of this project. Additional sums will not be awarded, and no overheads of any kind shall be approved. One of my men will be waiting for you at the airport with an advance of half a million US dollars. In accordance with your request, the financial aspect shall be handled strictly between the two of us, and no one else."

Assaf bid his host and the aides farewell, giving each a firm handshake, but not before he received the number of Shibu's direct line. A tall, broad-shouldered man was waiting for him at the airport. He gave Assaf a heavy black bag, which he transferred on board his plane without any inspection, taking it with him directly to his seat in first class. Assaf opened the bag only once he sat comfortably in his armchair with a glass of fine wine. He shut the bag the moment he opened it. He didn't have to count the money. He knew he could trust Shibu.

CHAPTER 17

Benino Impalo, or "the Colonel", as his close friends called him, served as Jeronti's military attaché in London. A personal appointment by President Imru, he made the leader's acquaintance back in the days of the militia. Impalo was a colonel in the government's army, until he came to the conclusion he could no longer abide the corruption and the mismanagement that resulted from it. One day, he defected, in full uniform, and made his way through the jungle directly into the militia's lines. Imru's men were astonished to find an officer in the government's army emerge from the trees. He asked them to take him to their commander, which they did.

- I stand before you, chief, ready and willing to serve you and your goal, which is no doubt to free Jeronti from the rule of corruption and take the country to a new path.

Handsome and tall, Impalo not only cut a dashing figure, he was also gregarious and captivating.

- How am I to know you're not here to spy on us? Do you know what we do to spies?

- Well, you cannot *know*. You can only choose to believe me, chief. I would like to further tell you, sir, that there are many officers who feel as I do, who are all waiting for you to take over and drive this gang of degenerates out.

Mkume Imru threw his arms around Impalo in a heartfelt embrace and made him a member of his high command.

Impalo proved highly capable and instrumental in the framework of the militia's captured of Golasa, so much so, that he distinguished himself. Once Imru assumed power and became president, he began ridding the establishment of the former government's men, including the removal of all the chiefs of Jeronti's diplomatic missions abroad.

One day, the president summoned Impalo. "I would like you to assume this mission for me. I am sending you abroad, to serve at our embassy in London, where we have numerous economic and military interests to cultivate. I only recently appointed a new ambassador, but he is busy with the diplomatic side of things, whereas I would like someone I truly trust to handle the most important issues. That is why you're going to serve as the military attaché at the embassy."

CHAPTER 18

Brosslav Lazienka was born in Zenica, the fourth largest city of Bosnia and Herzegovina. His life and times deserve a book of their own, and perhaps it shall indeed be written someday. He was quite young when he decided to leave his war-torn homeland and relocate. His friends told him about this place in Africa, Jeronti, where the streets are paved in gold. Also according to them, it never snowed there, which was another selling point.

Brosslav ended up in Jeronti at the end of a long and winding road. It was hot and humid. After a few nights at a fleabag motel, he decided to find the nearest bar and get to the bottom of why it is that there aren't any diamonds rolling in the streets, as promised.

"There's no money to be had 'round here. It's up north, where the oil is," a random drinking buddy informed him.

The very next day, Brosslav boarded a train. It was so packed, he couldn't even find a seat, so he had to stand for twelve hours and relieve himself by the side of the road like everyone else during the few short stops along the way. All those hard twists and bends and standing so long 'til his bones hurt served as a rude awakening that he needed a serious and rapid change. He decided to get off at the next stop, his resolve enforced by the image of this large tank, suggesting this was indeed the promised land.

When the train left Brosslav realized he was standing at the far end of this dusty village with poor looking huts on either side of the only dirt path there. He got closer to the inscription he saw from afar and was told he could get a bed in exchange for one dollar. He hardly needed any time to consider, and quickly laid himself to rest, his body aching from the journey.

Brosslav was suddenly woken by the sound of shots being fired. He didn't know long he had slept for. Seconds later, this dark man in battle fatigues, Kalashnikov in hand, stormed into his room. He could see the gentleman's finger was about to pull the trigger. When he would recount this story in later years, Brosslav would swear he saw the man's finger locking on the weapon, but then recoiling within a split second. The soldier thought better and kicked Brosslav out of the room. Next thing Brosslav recalls is the corpses piling up in the street, the cries of the injured, more dark-skinned gentlemen pulling girls out from every village hut and their fellow uniformed comrades shooting any other man they came across.

The soldiers kept shouting "Boko Haram! Boko Haram!"

They led Brosslav into the same square where they gathered those girls. Acutely aware he was the only white person around, he caught a glimpse, in the corner of his eye, three soldiers, probably the commanders of the raiding force, debating what to do with him, occasionally pointing at him. Eventually, they pushed him onto this truck that parked nearby, which drove them to a remote clearing in middle of the jungle.

- You, English?

Brosslav saw this tall man with silver hair on either side of his head and multiple scars, a chain of bullets across his chest and two boys with Kalashnikovs right behind.

- Yes. Me English.

It was then and there it dawned on him that his life could be saved thanks to the broken English that Gospodica (Miss) Irena, his teacher back at the Zenica elementary school, had taught him. Boko Haram, this murderous Muslim terrorist rebel organization, required his services as a translator.

During his years in captivity, Brosslav wrote letters for the rebels in his broken English and even translated letters for them into English. He toiled along with them, suffered from chronic hunger as they did and almost never spent more than one night at the same place. He took to praying five times a day facing Mecca, nevertheless without grasping a single word of what he was reciting. He witnessed countless atrocities these terrorist rebels perpetrated, from mistreatment of those girls through "plain" murders to horrid abuses. All that may indeed be put pen to paper someday.

Four years went by, until one day, shots covered the rebel camp, followed by swarms of dozens of soldiers in different uniforms who stormed in and killed anyone on sight.

"We are here to rescue you!" they told the captives.

Crying women and girls emerged from the jungle and ran at the soldiers, who in turn proceeded to take them away, Brosslav included, aboard their nearby trucks, right after setting the rebel camp on fire.

They reached the capital city after an eight-hour journey by road. The now freed captives met these women who presented themselves as relief workers on behalf of this English charity dedicated to rehabilitating Boko Haram victims. These charitable ladies were aided by local social and welfare workers. They couldn't be more surprised at the sight of Brosslav, but they nevertheless soon took to him and like the rest, he too was given medical attention and later clothes as well as a place to stay.

A few days later, the main office sent for Brosslav. They were situated in the same place he was housed. The British work aid told him:

- We looked into a few options of helping you out. We've got two suggestions. We can help you get back to your home country, or, if you like, send you to the UK, where you can get refugee status, a temporary legal stay. If this is your choice, we can give you references to hand over to our HQ in the UK. They'll help you find employment in England.

- I do prefer London, miss.

*

- Can you drive?

This was the very first question the security officer at the embassy of Jeronti asked Brosslav when he showed up for his job interview there.

- I've got an international driver license, but I don't know how to drive on the left-hand side of the road, sir.

- That's not a problem. We'll send you on a course. Once you pass the test, we'll be happy to engage your services as a chauffeur. The embassy driver got his license revoked for good, so we need a new driver.

'Bro', as the embassy staff took to calling him, worked there for five years until the military attaché sent for him one day. By then, he gained the affection of every employee. Many of them sent him on all sorts of errands, so he soon became highly familiar with London's roads. One of his most frequent drives was from the international airports surrounding the capital,

Heathrow, Gatwick, Stansted and Luton, picking embassy guests on arrival to the UK in the official car and carrying luggage and all sorts of packages, some of which he was asked never to talk about.

Jeronti's military attaché continued.

- So, Bro, I've got a mission for you. I'd like you to be a part of it based on the trust I place in you. Nevertheless, I need you to promise me two things. First. That you never, ever, tie me to this conversation or mention my name, and second, that once you complete this mission, you pocket the fifty thousand British Pounds I am going to give you and disappear from the UK for good. You have twenty-four hours to give me your answer.

Brosslav missed his family and friends back in Bosnia. He hadn't seen them for years and thought about them very often. Leaving the UK was hardly a new idea. He had entertained it many times.

Brosslav returned to the military attaché the following day and told him thus:

- I accept both terms.

- Good. The mission involves transporting a comatose man from the center of London to Stansted Airport. Your role is merely to drive the car. My friends from Israel will see to everything else. I took it upon myself to place a highly capable driver at their disposal, someone whose performance is no less than flawless. No screwups, nothing to offer "explanations" for. I know you're the right man.

- Thanks. What do I have to do?

- First thing tomorrow morning, you hire a simple car. We'll start practicing the drive from the designated pick up location to Stansted. I want to be involved in the planning of this route.

And indeed, the very next day, Brosslav and the military attaché walked up and down Walton Street and its surroundings, checking the traffic lights, the parking bays, private driveways and any other relevant detail they could think of. Then, they drove along the freeway that connects London to the highway system linking between the metropolis and its airports, making sure they get the timetable right. When they arrived at Stansted Airport, they made a note of the exits and entrances, the security measures, the parking lots and the road to the cargo terminal. They also made a note to get a detailed map of the airport. When they completed their arduous day, Bro returned his rental car and had a pint of beer with the military attaché.

- Tomorrow, I plan to rent another car and make the journey all over again, by myself this time.

- We count on you. One of the Israelis, a guy called Dudi, will call you sometime. He would like to get to know you in person.

- Sure. I would like to meet him.

*

Eli Alon was sitting in a café on Oxford Street. His gray tweed business suit complimented his tall figure and he blended very well into the crowd of attorneys and businessmen around him. All he wanted was black coffee and a fresh croissant, just like he was accustomed to ordering at the small coffee shop near his own Tel Aviv apartment on King George Street. Nevertheless, duty calls, so he asked for bacon and toast. 'When in Rome...,' he thought to himself. Then, this tall, dark elegant man with handsome features and a fine suit sat next to Eli. The man's extraordinary good looks attracted the attention of everyone there.

- My name is Benino Impalo. I'm from the embassy.

- Gadi from King George.

Eli's guest laughed out loud.

- Gadi? Very well, but 'King George'? Surely you could have come up with something better or more original!

- Ok, never mind about Gadi, but 'King George' - I'll have you know that's for real.

They shared a wholehearted lough and proceeded to discuss London and its numerous delights while they waited for the other people at the coffee shop to return to their respective offices after lunch.

- I've got what you had asked for. This file comprises the details we gathered from the architect who built the house Biko currently resides in. We also have the list of neighbors for you. Better note the third house on the left: it belongs to the Russian intelligence service. There are two more housed between their house and Biko's. One belongs to an Indian millionaire who is away in India for most of the year, and the other is home to a couple of pensioners. We found nothing remarkable in any of the other houses.

- Oh, Okay.

- Now, as for Biko's medical file. It's only partial, as gathering the data proved difficult, on top of costing us an arm and a leg. From what we were able to glean, he is as healthy as an ox. Fit, seldom sees any doctor. I believe what the file contains should suffice.

- Thanks for both files. Now, what about the car?

- We've arranged everything per your request. The same goes for the transfer of our 'client' from the car on board the cargo plane. You're going to like the solution we've come up with. As agreed, we'll provide you with all the details a short while before the operation starts.

- Sounds good, but we would like to see the driver before-hand and rehearse the escape route with him.

- Not a problem. I'll give you the number for the driver. His name's Brosslav. Your friend can coordinate with him once he's in London.

- We're counting on you. And now I have to hurry and catch my flight back to Tel Aviv.

- Thank you for coming all the way from King George. Quite an honor. My regards to Assaf. I hear he's a nice guy.

*

Dudi remembered Assaf's recommendation, so he arranged to meet "Bro" at Sweeny Bar, not far from Leicester Square.

Brosslav shook him by the hand

- It's me.

- I know. How are things coming along?

Dudi felt this was a man after his own heart the moment they shook hands. "Bro" told him about all the preparations and rehearsals he and the military attaché had made in the area designated for the operation, as well as the preparations he made on his own at various times during the day. Brosslav proceeded to show Dudi the map of Stansted Airport and briefed him on the access roads into and escape routes out of the airfield. He also briefed him on the availability of rental vehicles in each of the car hire companies there.

- Would you like to go on a test drive and check the scene out?

- Thanks. I am satisfied you're ready.

Dudi and Bro shook hands firmly and parted.

*

- How did your meetings in London go?

Dudi answered Assaf's question first.

- We can proceed.

Eli then added:

- I agree. At any rate, we're going to pay another visit to the scene right before we go.

- Excellent. Each of you three will arrive in London separately. I am going to give you an Israeli phone number. Call this number on Friday between four and six pm, and you'll receive the last details and the exact pickup location. Needless to say, you're only using a pay phone. Good luck to us all!

*

Dr. Dmitry Blog shut his office door and opened the envelope he received a short while earlier. '*What a small file. So little medical data to go on*'.

"That's all they managed to put together in London," Assaf told him before they parted.

'*I couldn't care less about his PSA or colonoscopy*,' Dima thought. '*Oh, that's more like it. His EKG and blood pressure are fascinating. Not bad for a fifty-year old man!*'

Dima and Assaf met again the following day at the hospital cafeteria.

- Well, they could have given me more to go on, but that's enough for me. We can continue.

- Excellent. What more do you need, Dima?

- Before I answer in detail, I've got an important request.

- Name it.

- The whole thing has to take place before noon time.

- Why is that?

- I would think it's a bit much to ask our "client" to fast, so the only alternative is to meet up with him when he's on an empty stomach, as empty as possible.

- Got it. What else?

- I hope you didn't neglect to bring me a chair comfortable to sit on for the duration of the flight.

- Everything shall be taken care of.

Prior to their partying, Assaf handed him a closed white envelope. When Dima opened it, he found ten thousand dollars, much to his excitement. Until then the largest sum he had ever held in his hands were the two thousand bucks he had stashed at his and Paulina's apartment back in Moscow. '*It's going to happen!*'

When the day drew to a close, he saw Assaf waiting for him at the end of the corridor. Dima invited him in, shut the door behind them and locked it.

- You need to be in London this coming Tuesday. Do not take a direct flight there. Your first lag must not be through Moscow, either. I assume you'll be absent from work for about seven days. Tell no one where it is you're going and do not take any luggage. A backpack should do. Book a room at a mediocre hotel in the center of London and move to another hotel the following day. Never leave your passport at the reception desk. Also, do not use a credit card. Make any payment strictly in cash. Never lose sight of your medical kit. Remember, the success of the entire operation depends on you. This is a phone number. Call it this Friday between four and six pm for further instructions. This is also your emergency number. Any questions or requests?

- Everything's clear, except for one thing. If anything should happen to me, will anyone know where I am and what-

- Don't worry. First of all, we're doing our utmost to make sure nothing happens. Second, you're working with highly responsible people. We do not leave friends behind. It's all going to be fine. I never forgot about the million dollars. They'll be waiting for you when you get back. Good luck in London!

Whether Dima had any doubts, misgivings or concerns as to the path his life was about to take, he left them all behind. *'There's clearly no way back. No regrets, certainly not with "friends" like that'.* He has been calculating the actions he was going to take and the stages at which he would take them. *'The moment has come. According to the data they've given me, the subject is a healthy man, fifty years old, who's supposed to go under for eleven hours, no less'.* Dima had already performed hundreds of anesthesia procedures, but this time was different. This is a forced sedation on the field with radical changes in the patient's status. *'This is going to be my first time doing this without any medical or professional assistance'.* Apprehensive, Dima recalled in horror the medical debacle in Moscow, despite having at his disposal a full medical team of doctors and auxiliary nurses and technicians. *'This time, I am on my own. It's just me and him. Our fates are bound together'.* His work had taught him to refer to any patient as though he was merely a "medical subject" rather than this human being whose soul he was about to "borrow" on a temporary basis. Dima never inquired after the patient's identity. The Moscow precedent, in the framework of which he had prior knowledge who was going to be sedated, plagued him. This time, he was bothered enough to feel sympathy for Biko. *'Here's a man, walking dully along down his street in London, and all of the sudden, they pounce, drag him to a car, and it's up to me to put him under, help take his liberty from him and watch over as he's been taken away, unconscious, to another continent. Does he have any family? Wife? Kids? Friends? A man just vanishes into thin air and no one's the wiser? Maybe I'm taking all this too far'.*

Dima made himself sedate his own thoughts and focused on the task at hand, going over the checklist he had already prepared. *'I have several options to perform the anesthesia. Still, the first few seconds are crucial. They'll determine everything that follows. We obviously mustn't undermine the element of surprise. On top of that, I need to put him out instantly, without any struggle. I'd better use Ketalar. Its main benefit is that its effect is immediate. No adverse effect on respiration. Yes. Three syringes should be enough, but I'd have spares all the same just to be on the safe side. I should also allow for the transfer from the car to the box and then on to the plane. According to the timetable they've given me, it's four hours from the moment we abduct him to the moment we strap him to the bed on board. The longest lag is the flight between London and Jeronti's capital, that's another seven some hours'.*

Dima's experience had taught him that long, sound and stable sleep calls from administering the sedative intravenously, so he made a note to himself to have a dose of Propozole ready to inject into the man's vein. He further added he should have a monitor at hand, to monitor the patient's status at all times, a balloon inflation device, complete with a mask in case of any difficulty breathing, as well as tranquilizer pills. Before he completed his list, Dima added a knife and sharp scissors, in order to allow him smooth and rapid access to the patient's vein, if it should come to it.

'I know how to get hold of all that. Unlike Moscow, where everything was under lock and key, complete with accurate inventory lists. But in Israel, it's all available to the medical staff.

Sure enough, the very next day, when he was done with his duties attending on surgeries, Dima placed all the medical equipment and supplies he needed in his bag. *'Ready. Here I go'.*

*

Eli came over on a red eye fight from Amsterdam. He caught some z's at the airport hotel and made his way on to Heathrow to London by train, disembarking at Westminster station, where he got on the tube to Southbank. He soon found himself a small hotel close to the south bank of the Thames, where they weren't too particular about keeping an exact record of the guests. Once he settled in at his modest lodgings, he went down to the nearest pay phone and placed a call to Jeronti's military attaché.

Mary, the attaché's faithful secretary, put the call through right away.

- My hotel is right by the tube station on Southbank.

- Excellent. Makes it easier for me to get to you without having to use my official car. I'll be there in about an hour.

Impalo showed up in plain clothes. One embrace and a few pleasantries later, he and Eli walked along the river embankment and relished the unseasonably fair sky. They came across this café and sat at the exterior terrace overlooking Westminster Abbey across the Thames.

- Everything's ready for you three. We only need to iron out the last few details. Let's get breakfast out of the way first, I'm starving.

- That makes two of us. I haven't had a bite since yesterday.

Their breakfast arrived at exactly the right time and both burly men devoured their eggs and bacon. Once they had their plates cleared, they got on to the matter at hand.

- The Boeing will arrive at Stansted on Monday night.

- Why did you pick this airport? Isn't Heathrow safer?

- We chose Stansted for lots of reasons. It is indeed further away from London, but access is easier, thanks to the North Circular Road and the M11 highway. Given that it's considered a peripheral airport, Stansted has less control, so it's more lax. In addition, Jeronti's government has its own cargo terminal there, so we can set the pane's exact location for the layover. As you can see, this offers us free access to it.

- What do you mean?

You gave us to problems to solve: one - how to allow the extraction vehicle undisturbed access right to the aircraft's entrance, given the cargo area is a closed and well-monitored space; second, how to get approval from both customs and security to have the box on board, with the people inside, without inspection. We solved both issues: you shall have free access to the terminal. We've got that taken care of, and at quite a high cost, mind you. The second problem proved trickier, but we've got that sorted as well.

- Well done! I am truly impressed. Do go on.

- The British customs authorities are sticklers for details. They work by the book. Literally. You cannot get anything on board, not so much as a pin, without their clearance, signatures on numerous forms and so on, least of all a sedated person with another man standing by with an IV and two others guarding them, keeping the guy from waking up. Actually, the reason isn't the fact that there's anything illegal about this, but simply because their manual doesn't mention anything like that. They simply don't have a clause covering this type of situation.

Both men laughed and Impalo continued.

- The issue of security is also a tricky point. They're keeping a close eye on everything, now more than ever, so there is no way they would allow a big closed box onto any aircraft without checking its contents first, as carefully as they possibly can.

Eli hummed in agreement.

- So we've come up with a special solution thanks to President Imru's intervention. He gave his approval, so be extra careful not to fk this up: according to the bilateral treaty between the UK and Jeronti, diplomatic parcels have immunity from inspection. The box shall bear the seal of diplomatic mail and be placed on board the plane by virtue of this exemption. It's up to me to stamp it, so be nice. I suggest you cover the check for breakfast, or I might forget about showing up at the airport...

Eli paid their bill.

- Oh, I see my warning helped. I'll take care of the tip. See you tomorrow.

A moment before he was about to leave, Impalo added:

- I nearly forgot: this is Brosslav's phone number. Yes, the driver. He's a good chap. He's expecting your call. Make all the arrangement with him directly.

Right after the meeting, Eli switched to another hotel. If his basic intelligence course way back when had told one thing, it was that routine is the menace of reconnaissance. He chose the West End as the location of his next lodging, seeing as this dense theater and entertainment district is chockfull of pubs, restaurants and multitudes one can easily disappear into when need be. Another advantage the new digs afforded him was the proximity, a five minute walk in fact, from Leicester Square, where he and Dudi had arranged to meet at the Irish pub at five o'clock.

*

"I'm going away to Paris for a few days," Dudi kissed his wife and left.

He boarded a flight to Copenhagen at the airport, managed to catch a last minute flight to London, and took a taxi from Heathrow straight to a down town Hilton. The hotel reception desk received Dudi's French passport. He spent very little time getting settled at his luxury suite, after which he came right back down, helped himself to a detailed map of London, with an emphasis on the immediate vicinity, the center of London, and out he went.

*

"Never stay at fancy hotels, do not ever leave your passport back at the hotel, avoid using your credit cards, and also, you must never use the phone in your room." Those were the instructions Assaf had given Dudi the last time they met back in Israel. The latter did heed them: he did not leave his Israeli passport behind and carried around lots of cash, never forgetting that using the room phone was strictly for people who have absolutely nothing to hide. The only thing he did not adhere to, was the level of his hotel, as he simply could not abide by any less than his creature comforts. '*What harm could a three-day stay at the Hilton do to the entire operation?*' he told himself. Another concession took the form of a simple old plaid shirt, rather than the brand name attire Dudi usually sported, in addition to baggy pants and an old tweed jacket. He put on an old cap and dark sunglasses. '*Even the police detectives back in Netanya would never recognize me,*' he noted, satisfied at the sight of his getup in the mirror

Walking down Oxford Street, Dudi couldn't help gazing at his image in the shop windows every now and then. Force of habit. He was accustomed to looking over his shoulder and looking out for any possible surveillance. On occasion, he would join the groups of tourists who huddled together in and around the various places and submerged himself in them, only to continue on his own a few moments later. Eventually, Dudi arrived by tube at Baker Street station, where he switched trains en route to East Side, where he emerged to take the first taxi he hailed and instructed the cabbie to take him to No. 60 Walton Street. When he got out of the cab, he inspected his surroundings very closely and at length until he was satisfied no one was following him.

No. 14 was only twenty-three houses further away, up the road. Dudi began walking in this direction, examining the neighborhood as he was approaching. The street itself was quite in line with his expectations: an aristocratic line of classy two-story houses, many of which attached, complete with their own parking spaces up front. The houses further up the road were fancier still, some standing apart from one another. A red phone booth was located near No. 40. Dudi walked in and called his hotel. When he heard the line, he hung up. '*The pay phone is working*'. He proceeded to sit by this nearby bench and looked on, wishing to gauge how many people were using the public phone, and how often. '*Not a single soul for thirty minutes*'. The street itself was wide, but the sidewalks quite narrow, frequented by very few pedestrians. The view was clear all across. So much so, that Dudi could see No.14 from as far as where he was sitting.

'*I'd better leave inspecting the house for another visit,*' he decided. While he was sitting on the bench, he could see, further up Walton Street, some ten houses further, an iron gate opening, through which this black Bentley exited. It had foreign license plates. When it passed Dudi by, he spotted a chauffeur in uniform and a man in a three-piece suit sitting in the back seat. He managed to make a note of the number without being noticed.

'Better safe than sorry'.

Dudi and Eli met at the Irish pub at five pm. Were it not for their prior acquaintance, Eli would never have recognized the man in those old tweed getup, plaid cap, round vintage glasses and a grand mustache. *'I've got a lot to learn from him,'* he thought as he invited Dudi to his table.

Eli then turned to the waitress in a perfect cockney accent:

- Two beers please, miss.

- So how was your tour?

- Very informative, Eli. I suggest we both pay a visit there tomorrow before noon, to determine the exact time we nab our guy.

*

The following day at eleven, two French tourists were seen walking down Walton Street. Those who came across these two, immediately guessed they were architects, seeing as one, who looked quite elegant, was explaining to the other, in perfect French, about the British style of building the various houses in the immediate vicinity were good examples of. The other tourist didn't say a word. Who was only taking pics of these structures.

The two met again at the Hilton bar.

- So it's agreed. House number twenty.

*

The cargo plane was waiting, engines still running, on the runway at the airport near Golasa, Jeronti's capital. The captain was John Mkombo, and his co-pilot was Jimmy Modo.

"Flight plan for number seven one nine to London is cleared," the tower told the captain, who proceeded to taxi, accelerate and take off, direction: north-west.

The previous evening, the chief of operations at Jeronti's national airline company summoned captain Mkombo and apprised him of the importance of the flight he was entrusting to his capable hands. Upon his customary inspection prior to takeoff, Mkombo spotted a large box riveted to the floor. Having served as a senior commander in Jeronti's air force, he knew all too well there was little point in asking questions he wasn't about to get any answers to.

Mkombo radioed upon crossing the channel:

- Hello Stansted control. This is flight 719.

- I see you. Come down to twenty-two thousand feet and follow the instructions.

- Roger that.

- Prepare for landing. Direction: south-west. Wind speed: 10 knots.

- Roger.

- Good landing, mate. Welcome to England. Taxi on all the way to the end of your runway.

- Roger. Over.

- Ground control to flight 719.

- Read you loud and clear. Over.

- Clear the runway. Turn left and continue to Diamond Terminal. Your designated slot is number 42.

As soon as he stopped the engines, Mkombo saw a large cargo forklift approaching his plane's back exit. He proceeded to open the bay door per the previous instructions he was given. The forklift carried the box out using its two huge iron teeth and placed it next to the aircraft. A moment later, a large tanker appeared and began to fuel his plane. Mkombo and his co-pilot remained on board and awaited further instructions.

*

The previous day, "Bro" took the train from London to Stansted, where he rented a van for the following three days, for which he paid in cash. He drove the van to the center of London and parked it in a public parking lot, from which he returned home by tube.

The next day, Brosslav took the van from the parking lot, picked Dudi up at ten to eight in the morning at the corner of Piccadilly and Coventry. He picked Eli up two minutes later on the corner of Regent St. He then picked another gentleman up a few yards later. This gentleman was carrying a large black bag. Bro then continued on to Walton St. Seeing as he was five minutes ahead of schedule, he stopped the van by the side of the road and kept the engine running.

They saw Biko at half past eight exactly when he embarked on his morning constitutional. Bro lifted his foot from the breaks, approached him, climbed the pavement and cut off Biko's path.

CHAPTER 19

Bwana Biko was a creature of habit. So much so, he was a stickler for his habits, in particular his morning walks and the attire he designated for them. He relished the western side of his street. During one of his first mornings in the new digs, he discovered, much to his surprise, that even in London the sun also shines sometimes, and on those rare occasions, it's the western side of Walton Street that receives the first rays. Should the sun persist, the eastern bank too receives its share, however tentative. This was the moment he developed a preference for the western side. The house he'd bought was situated to the right of Walton, as was the neighboring mansion, "Tea House", which he believed owed much of its appearance to its exposure to the sun. This was no doubt the case with the blooming rose beds right next door.

Biko always wore the same outfit on his morning constitutionals. During one of his very first meetings with Attorney Byrot, he told him about his addiction to morning walks. The esteemed attorney advised Biko he would have to reconcile himself to English weather and sent him to one of his friends, head of the sports department at Harrods, where Biko was soon fitted with comprehensive attire for outdoor sports, from "Kylie pants", through to a water resistant Adidas overcoat to a pair of Nikes size 12. Nevertheless, once Biko confided in him he had a sore ankle, the manager promised him he would find him customized shoes with matching soles. Biko left the store with two identical sets of outfits and was awarded a special gift in the form of a dual layer gray wool cap with red and yellow stripes.

That morning was no exception. Biko waited for his secretary to arrive, greeted her as usual, and off he went, his "good morning" still reverberating.

*

Dr. Blog was sitting in the van's back seat, anxious and alert, clutching the syringe. The back door was open. A few seconds after Brosslav stopped it on the pavement, screeching, Dima's friends dragged a heavy-set man in, gagged his mouth with some wide band and covered his eyes with a black bandage. 'What a tantrum,' Dima thought to himself as Biko was throwing his arms in the air, desperately to break free from the two strongmen's clutch.

It took Dudi but a second to produce zip ties to bind Biko's hands to the fronts seat's metal leg. The abducted man was flinging his legs ferociously about now, so Eli quickly cuffed them. Dudi sat on Biko's head and forced his hands together in an iron grip.

This was the doctor's que, the moment he was waiting for. He held the shot closer to Biko's arm. Realizing the "client" had on a thick jersey jacket, he quickly produced a scalpel, cut the sleeve across and injected him with Ketalar through the thin shirt, straight to the vein. Biko was out like a light even before Dr. Blog pulled the syringe out. The subject froze instantly and fell into this deep sleep, from which he was to awaken no sooner than fourteen hours later, in the heart of Africa.

Dudi and Eli were sitting on the floor of the van, all sweaty and tense. Each of them felt his heart pounding and tried to regulate his breathing. Although the whole abduction took only one hundred seconds, they were both feeling like they had just run a marathon. They moved to the back seat, leaving the doctor alone with Biko. Dima never took his eyes off the patient, occasionally taking his blood pressure.

Brosslav merged with the relatively calm morning traffic, making sure he wasn't attracting any undue attention. After about forty minutes, he merged to the acceleration lane and continued on the North Circular Road. An hour later, the M11 highway brought them to Stansted Airport, where they headed straight for the cargo terminal.

The van stopped in front of an iron gate, which then opened right away. The security guard was undoubtedly expecting them. Bro drove all the way to the end of the terminal, where this Boeing 707 cargo plane with Jeronti's insignia was waiting. Over by the back, they saw a large box, but there was no one there. Furthermore, no one made contact with them. Dudi saw that the cockpit wasn't empty, but still, no one attempted to make any contact with them. The van backed up and reached the box.

Eli got off the van and opened its back door. He and Dudi lifted the sedated Biko by his arms and legs and transported him into the box, where they laid him on the bed that stood at the center of the box, riveted to its floor with iron rings. They proceeded to tie Biko to the bed's iron chains using the fitted leather straps.

The box also had a cushioned chair by the bed and another

chair behind it. Doctor Blog went in and checked Biko's blood pressure again. Eli entered the box right behind Dima and sat on the chair behind.

Dudi turned to Bro.

- I'm not coming along. I decided to stay behind with the guys. You can go now.

Bro motioned "thumbs up" and drove the van to Stansted's center. He parked at the lot designated for rentals, right next to the airport's main offices, and returned the keys to the drop-box with the car hire company's sign that indicated its purpose. Brosslav then made his way to the passenger terminal and went in the direction of the "Departures" signs. Two hours later, he ordered a glass of red wine aboard a plane, the moment they were crossing the channel en route the continent. He gave a toast and vowed there and then never to return to London.

*

The box sported high walls and plenty of room. Its measurements were fitted to the cargo planes back door. Its distinct walnut scent indicated it was completed very recently. The floor of the box had several power outlets next to the bed, over which stood a large light bulb. Rather than a water closet, the box featured a water tank in the corner.

Dudi also went into the box, right after Bro drove the van away and left. As Biko was already bound to the bed, Eli shut the door, locking all four men in.

- Why didn't you leave with Bro? According to our plan, you were supposed to go straight to the passenger terminal and board the first flight out of Britain.

- I changed my mind, Eli. Everything went so well. They're

going to load us on board in no time and take off for Jeronti.

- But you have no room to sit. Don't expect me to give up my chair for you.

- Don't sweat it. After all, after they place us in, we'll open the door and I'll find a seat on board. I can't wait to piss.

- I can't wait to have a drink. I gather that we'll be flying within fifteen minutes from our arrival, so we'll be up soon. I also understood there's plenty to drink and eat inside, too. Either way, I think that even as the plan did go smoothly so far, you still should have adhered to it and returned to Israel.

- There's another reason for my decision to arrive to Jeronti on board this plane, Eli.

- Yeah? Why is that, Dudi?

- I want to make sure no one makes a fool out of us.

- Whatever do you mean?

- Look, Eli, as much as it's true we didn't do it just for the money, and I'm speaking mainly for myself here, still, I am not forgetting, not for one second, that each of us is due to receive one million US dollars in exchange for our respective parts. I am sure this sum matters to you a great deal. To Doctor Dima, too, eh? What do you say, doc?

- Are you nuts? Do you honestly think I would have joined this f***ed up operation, risked my life and losing my medical license were it not for one million bucks? I used to think this is a huge sum, but I'm not so sure anymore.

- Dudi, what's come over you? Are you worried about the money? What's the problem?

- Don't worry, Eli. This 'cargo' we've got here is worth a great deal. It's just that I've learned never to trust anyone. Only myself. Where are they? I really need to go…

- And I really need to have something to drink. What are

you dying for, doc?

- I can't wait to hand over my patient, collect what's due to me and return home.

- Is that all? Dudi, I have to say I trust you and Assaf completely. It's the fact that you prefer this box inside a f******g cargo plane over a business class seat that's beginning to worry me. I can't wait to have a sip of water!

- I do trust Assaf. Even more than that, I am counting on his integrity. I'm also counting that he knows I am not to be messed around with. Anyone who has, ended up under a different kind of sedation.

- It's been an hour already, and nothing's going on. I'd be forced to go right here in this box in five minutes.

- Don't you dare! It's all well for Eli and you, you two are done, but I still have my work. We must keep the box clean and hygienic, sterile, even. If anything should happen to him, those Africans will pay us nothing. I'm getting nervous as it is. The injection I gave him is good for two hours. After this, I thought of giving him a different shot. Better do this under the best conditions.

- So you've got another half hour, by which time we'll be on the plane, I'm sure. But I do not even have five minutes. Either I go right here or wet myself.

- Here's a plastic bag. After you're done, seal it tight and place it in that corner.

Dudi relieved himself.

- Now that Dudi has solved his own great matter, let's return to our small issues. What makes you think you need to arrive to Jeronti with 'the client'?

- Frankly, I don't know how the payment is actually going to be made. I understood from Assaf, it's 'goods for cash', so the moment the person we've abducted reaches the airport, we each get our dues.

- So why did you originally think of traveling from London to Israel? According to my arrangement with Assaf, he will receive the payment and deposit my share in my own Swiss bank account. That should solve all sorts of questions at Ben Gurion Airport.

- The bag is already full, but nothing seems to be happening.

- What are you doing, doctor?

- Time is passing, and I am not about to inject him with another shot of Ketalar, because if I do, you're going to have to kidnap him again.

- But weren't you going to administer a different sedative?

- True, but I haven't got the proper conditions for that. I'm going to give him a small dose, which I will later augment with another dose once we're in the air.

- As long as you don't kill our meal ticket.

- Given the payment arrangement, what makes our money secure?

- That's exactly what I asked Assaf. He swore by our friend-ship, by the eyes of the beautiful Maya, who I used to love so much, and even by his honor as a Mossad commander, that we shall receive everything we are due.

- And was that enough for you?

- You'd better ask me later. Now, what is it, doc? I can see there's something on your mind again?

- That's right. We've been sitting in this box for three hours now, and nothing. I got a very well-structured plan from Assaf, on the basis of which I formed my own plan for the anesthesia. He told me we'd be flying within two hours at the most from the moment we kidnap this guy. I did allow for a little longer than that, but even according to my schedule, time is running out.

- Is that all?

- No. Something in my gut reminds me of a similar situation in Moscow a while back. That was years ago. It didn't end well.

- What happened?

- I was the anesthesiologist in the framework of an operation on a senior NKVD chief. He never woke from the surgery. I felt something was wrong. I didn't need the autopsy findings to know my gut feeling was right. I have the same feeling now. Seriously, something doesn't feel right.

- Interesting. Eli, what do you think about our situation?

- Where the devil is Impalo?

- Who's Impalo?

- He is the key person, doc. He's the embassy's security officer. He was supposed to see to it the box is cleared for loading on board.

- How was he to be notified the abduction was successful?

- While you were busy with your patient, I heard Bro, the driver, radio the embassy the operation was carried out and that we were on our way to the airport. Besides, maybe you weren't aware of this, we were being escorted this entire time by an embassy car. They stopped near a pay phone right after we kidnapped Biko. I saw them. They were supposed to call and report 'mission accomplished'.

- What an S.O.B indeed. But what are we to do now? Bear in mind it's already getting dark, and we don't even have light. Dudi, why are you so quiet all this time?

- If I'm not saying a word, that means I'm thinking.

- So what are you thinking about?

- I think we should not have counted on Impalo. But he isn't our problem. Our problem is Assaf. Eli and I were in charge of the extraction, which we carried out. We have delivered the goods. You have been in charge of sedating Biko, which is also done. So far so good. Assaf was in charge of coordinating everything that pertains to getting the box on board the cargo plane and as it would seem, there's a major problem here. Quite a fiasco.

- In that case, what are you going to do?

- I have a bone to pick with Assaf!

- Okay, but what are we going to do in the meantime?

- I looked out and saw the Boeing waiting on the tarmac. Bear in mind the crew probably does have contact with the embassy. They're probably pretty nervous too. In half an hour's time, in the cloak of darkness, I shall leave the box and go over there to see what's what. Don't forget sitting on the floor is hard on me too. It's been four hours. I'm running out of air, too.

Darkness descended. Biko was lying frozen, out like a log. The doctor was dozing off as well. Eli was silent and motionless in his chair. Dudi got up from the floor and made his way to the box's opening. That same moment, a miracle happened.

They heard voices from outside. This prompted Dima to say:

- They must have come to get us out.

The wooden wall was being hammered through. Then, two strong flashes lit the interior.

- How are you, boys?

- What took you so long? I am dying for something to drink!

- We have to get Biko on board right now!

A team of burly men pounced on the three. Before they could respond, they found themselves handcuffed and bound.

- Good evening. This is Scotland Yard.

CHAPTER 20

Sergeant Backboard was stroking his stubble and rubbing his red eyes. He took one last sip from his coffee mug and took a peek at the ledger. *'Nothing to report,'* he smiled, satisfied there was very little to pass on to the next shift. Two cases of theft, one count of sexual harassment, and eight complaints of car break-ins. The last event he entered in the report was Mrs. Smith lodging her serious protest against the neighbor's dog, who did its business in the park. *'Better leave that to the next shift. I'm done in five. It's home for me. A nice shower, some shut eye, and then: Arsenal vs Chelsea with my son'.* But the phone rang, cutting his musings short.

- Westminster station. Good morning, how may I help you?

- My boss is being kidnapped.

'Prank call? I'm not letting this loony interfere with my plans,' was all Sgt. Backboard could think of at first.

- Please calm down, madam. Now, please tell me who you are and what this is all about.

- My name is Edie. I work as the personal secretary of Minister Biko Bwana from Jeronti. Your chaps know all about him. Well, I just saw him being abducted!

- What did you see exactly?

- I was standing by the veranda and saw this car cut Biko

off. Two men came out, pounced on him and dragged him in.

- Where are you calling from?

As he was speaking, the sergeant pushed a button at the bottom of his desk, and a red list appeared on the screen before him, comprising the names of people under threat. Bwana Biko's name was among the top persons on this list. He noticed the star next to his name, indicating that anything to do with that particular personage ought to be reported forthwith to so and so number at Scotland Yard, the British police.

- I'm at number fourteen Walton St. Come quick, I'm so worried!

- Stay put. We'll handle this right away.

Backboard sighed in relief as he dialed Scotland Yard. *'Those good old boys won't leave this matter to a local station. I shan't be missing Arsenal's game after all',* he thought.

As he had expected, the duty officer at the Yard thanked him for bringing the matter to their attention and told him they were on it from there on. Backboard made an entry of the call and the subsequent alert to the Yard in the ledger and passed the shift on to the next police officer who came to replace him. He hurried out, rushing home for fear of yet another complaint that might delay him, *'maybe someone wants to report a corpse at Westminster Abbey?'*

*

The commander on duty at the Yard sent a police car round to Walton Street. Upon their return, the reported as follows:

- This seems to be a valid complaint, so I hereby call a level three alert.

- What are the details?

- Very sketchy at the moment. The report refers to a gray van. The woman who called it in didn't get a chance to take the license plate number. She's sure there were two kidnappers. It all happened very fast, she says. She wasn't sure, but she thinks they were wearing masks. The van left the scene at a normal speed, no panic. Seems like an altogether highly professional job.

- What can you tell me about the woman who made the call?

- She's very excited, but she seems highly credible.

The commander on duty followed procedure and reported the event to the deputy chief of operations. The latter's response was immediate: all units within three miles from the area of the abduction were called in. The roadblocks that were soon set up stopped to inspect every gray van. They also alerted border control, who in turn began canvassing specific suspects in known hotspots. Three hours after that, they escalated the alert to level four, one level below emergency status.

The details of the event were soon brought to the attention of Scotland Yard Chief George McMillan, who in turn ordered intelligence to be beefed up. He also asked the situation room at the Foreign Office be notified. Shortly thereafter, the deputy secretary for African Affairs took a personal interest in Biko's case. Surprisingly, another call came from the office of the Governor of the Bank of England, who asked to be updated of any development. Journalists and TV news crews soon picked up the scent of some unusual event that was afoot, so they quickly huddled near Scotland Yard headquarters. McMillan's term as chief was up for renewal so he took no chances. He cleared his entire scheduled and devoted himself to the case, heading the search for Biko himself. McMillan ordered the search radius to be widened, and then extended further, to include airports as well.

*

Inspector John Clark arrived at the cargo terminal at Stansted in his police car, albeit wearing plain clothes. He stepped out and went over to an airport security guard standing by the gate.

- Have you seen any gray van entering the terminal in the past few hours?

- No.

Nevertheless, something about the way he replied bothered inspector Clark. Maybe it was the rapid dismissal or the guard's involuntary blink of an eye. It may well have been the hunch of an experienced officer. Either way, he thanked the guard, returned to his car and called his commander.

- There's something fishy going on at Stansted Airport, sir.

A quick inspection at the terminal revealed that a cargo plane belonging to Jeronti's government had been standing on the tarmac for twelve hours.

- Gotcha!

McMillan's hurrah echoed through the corridors. He then headed a team of eight police cars and made a dash for the airport. The stunned guard at the gate quickly raised the barrier, as he had been ordered to, and gazed at the sight of all those police cars racing in, heading for that Boeing cargo plane at the end of the terminal.

Next to the plane, the police force saw this great big box. It was shut from all sides. One of the officers brought a crowbar and used it to break one of the sides open. The sight was like something out of an Agatha Christie whodunit: a man lying on a bed, to which he was strapped. His eyes were open, but he was clearly somewhere else altogether. Next to him, there was a gentleman holding a syringe, his face the picture of shock and awe. Two other men were there. One was still sitting, and the other complained,

- What took you so long? We've been waiting for hours now.

These people could not be more shocked when their sudden 'guests' identified themselves as police officers, after which they cuffed the three at gun point.

Then, as they were being pushed into the police cars, this black Mercedes suddenly appeared. The driver was clearly amazed by all those police vehicles. He was about to make a U-turn and scram, but two cars blocked his path, one in front and one from the back. The driver was then obliged to step out, and as he did, he began waving his diplomatic passport about and yelled at the officers.

- I'm a diplomat! I have immunity, you can't stop me! You're violating my diplomatic status!

Unimpressed, the commander had him arrested there and then along with the others. "We'll get to the bottom of what you're getting up to, using your diplomatic *immunity!*"

The chief then called an ambulance and ordered the cars to block the plane on either side, thereby preventing its crew from escaping. Off the police cars went, along with the men arrested. A doctor and two medics stepped off the ambulance. They untied Biko and transported him to their ambulance using a gurney. Then, they raced to the nearest hospital, lights flashing and sirens howling.

CHAPTER 21

He was standing by her desk, tall, very good-looking and dark. He was the first person to greet her and receive her on her first day there. Her little hand even smaller in the huge palm of his hand. '*He was holding my hand for a long while there, or was I just imagining it?*' Later that day, when it so happened that she needed to have his signature for some power of attorney, she felt his long, strong arm on hers. Then, he pulled back after signing, still caressing her hers. This sensation of dark skin over white excited her greatly. So much so, that she gathered the papers as quick as she could, rushed back to her desk and sat, out of breath, hoping he did not spot her stirring emotions.

That night, Mary could not fall asleep: his dark, handsome face, his strong scent, the silky touch of his hand and his arm were too exciting and arousing. The very next morning, she came in early and spent the time until his arrival by sorting the overnight mail. Then, he greeted her when he came in, and she in turn offered him his morning coffee.

- No thank you. I do not take my coffee so early. But I would love a cup of Earl Grey, please.

When she came in to his office for his signature on a few documents, she once again felt the exquisite feeling of his silky touch, only that this time, his hand moved freely to her shoulders and caressed her lower back, all the way down to the crack between her butt cheeks. '*Does he sense how much I tremble?*' she wondered, while at the same time his quivering hand indicated to her what was about to play out.

The day was barely winding down. He never approached her, and she, in turn, didn't seem able to shift anything from her in box to her out box. When it finally turned five o'clock, she knocked on his door, as was her custom before leaving for the day. When he opened his office door, he kissed her on the lips, shoved a yellow post-it into her hand and said, "Nine o'clock".

Only two blocks away did Mary muster the nerve to open her clenched fists and peek at his note. He gave her his phone number and his address, a posh London borough. The moment she got home, she ran herself a bath, barely holding herself from jumping in the water in her clothes. Quite a while later, she got out of the bubbles and poured herself a glass of well chilled white wine. '*Two hours to go*'. She spotted her lingerie drawer and picked up a racy number she had picked up at this small, audacious boutique in Chelsea. The drawer on top of that one comprised of her regular Selfridges undergarments, which she would purchase when they were on sale. Sensible and mundane, she wore those on a daily basis as well as on the odd date. The racier kind were her constant form of solace on days of gloom and bust, all too painfully aware she could ill-afford them, seeing as for the price of one pair of slutty knickers from Chelsea, she could get four decent Selfridges undies. Nevertheless, she could not resist the silks and laces of sexy lingerie. Mary took her much loved items out of their dedicated drawer and laid them all on the bed, debating whether the black pair, the pink, the white, the striped or any of the others would suit her best.

When she would feel particularly lonely, Mary would try her lace knickers in front of the mirror until the sorry state abated somewhat. But as the years wore on, she grew ever more skeptical that any hands other than her own would caress her, let alone thrill her as much as her fine delicates did.

'*Today's the day*'. She felt so for sure. '*One hour to go*'. She looked at her bed, all covered in sexy lingerie, as far as the eye could see. '*The white ones it is, then. The black pair might have no luster against his ebony body. The pink ones? Too childish, too vanilla for our rendezvous. How 'bout the patterned ones? I'm not sure that's to his liking. White is the safest bet. The ultimate choice*'.

Relishing every second, Mary put her sexy undies on, one leg at a time. '*Soft lace and silk, handwoven by some Yugoslav seamstress. Well, at eighty pounds, they'd better be worth it*'. Her appearance made her feel she had made the deal of her lifetime when she bought them.

Right before she put on her matching bra, she felt her breasts. '*Will he notice?*' They were uneven. The left one was perkier, firmer and bigger, whereas the white seemed rather saggy. Mary felt too self-conscious to bring this up with her mother. Instead, she went to see her school counselor, who in turn did her best to set her mind at ease, telling her that was the same for most women, actually. Cathy from that shop in Chelsea got to see quite a bit of Mary's breasts.

"They're lovely, really," Cathy would often tell her, adding, "you should have no issues with them whatsoever, honestly. Besides, I'll be da***d if I ever saw any man sizing his girl-friend's bosom *before* laying his hands on them for the first time. Moreover, there's nothing a good bra can't sort".

'*Fifteen minutes*'. Mary put on a black dress with golden stripes and selected a pair of matching shoes. She then ran out to catch a cab. On arrival at the address she gave the cabby, she spotted a real live mansion. The large doorman was expecting her. He motioned her to take the elevator, which he held open. The door shut, and the elevator took her directly to the fifth floor. Mary didn't even push a single button. Stepping out, she saw the entire floor had only one door, which was slightly open. She didn't know whether to knock or take this as an invitation to simply come in.

- Oh, how lovely to see you here!

There was Benino Impalo, standing at the door, irresistible in that white robe of his, accentuating his dark body. '*The white pair was a good choice*,' she couldn't help thinking.

- What are you standing in the doorway for? Do come in!

The center of his living room sported a dining table with a white cloth, a fine dinner set for two, complete with superb silver. In addition to the cutlery, she spotted a wine bottle, which she was certain he had picked out all by himself, whereas the silverware came along with the catering service dinner, but Mary was left with no time for such idle thoughts, though, as they were both obviously keen, but not on the sumptuous meal...

Within seconds, at no further ado, Impalo held Mary in his strong arms. Next, he carried her to his bedroom. She didn't even recall getting out of her dress on the way to his bed, but she did pause to wonder whether he liked her choice of panties when he took them off of her. He didn't bother with her bra. She held his firm buttocks as he climbed on top. Only after their first session was over, did he remove her bra. '*Ah oh, what now?*' she nervously awaited his response.

Much to Mary's amazement, his lips couldn't get enough

of her right breast. When he had finally moved to her left one, she suddenly saw, for the first time, a perky, well-formed breast, with a lovely nipple crowning it. His lips left no part of her unattended. His delight with her body knew no end. '*Pity he didn't see my knickers, he would have loved them*'. That was the last time she minded about that, as the rush and gush of ecstasy filled her. Impalo, for his part, took great pleasure in delighting her, until they were both breathless and exhausted. Then, he turned on his back and Mary laid her head on his chest.

"I could use a day off tomorrow," she said sweetly, feigning a coy demeanor.

"Granted. I could do with short break myself," he echoed her chipper tone, albeit his was genuine.

They slept in, waking up as the sun reached its zenith by noon. It occurred to them they hadn't had anything to eat since the day before.

- I love your knickers, they're so lovely!

She put them back on, noting he didn't take any notice of her bra. Much to her disappointment, her right breast was saggy once again.

They found the dinner set just as they left it the night before. They ravaged their meal as they had done each other. Famished, they hadn't even bothered to heat it up. A short while later, they climbed each other once more, made ample use of Impalo's bed and fell asleep again.

*

- Benny, someone's at the door!

He woke and heard the knocking too.

- Who could this possibly be? I left specific instructions I was not to be interrupted! I told the security officer at the embassy I wouldn't be coming to work today.

Impalo put his white dressing gown on and went to answer the door.

- Who is this?

- It is I, Hamadou, from the embassy.

- What brings you over?

- Everyone's worried. They've been looking all over for you for hours. The pilots at the airport are frantic. They don't know what to do.

Shocked, Impalo ran back to his bedroom. *'How could I forget!?'* He put on the first item of clothing he laid his eyes on, grabbed the keys to his Mercedes and rushed out, not before telling Mary, "Go home. I'll call you."

'The road to the airport isn't supposed to take this long. What's with this traffic jam now?'

The afternoon traffic was heavy indeed. After quite a while of crawling at a glacial pace, Impalo finally arrived at Stansted Airport, where he made a quick turn towards the cargo terminal. *'The police at the terminal gate seem tougher than I remember'.* He quickly produced his diplomatic passport relieved to find it so quickly on his person. The guard left him and went to speak to someone on the phone, after which he raised the barrier and let him in.

Racing, Impalo could still see the Boeing parked at the end of the runway, with the box right next to it. Reassured, he sighed, growing even more relieved, and hit the brakes beside the big box.

- Out of the car, sir! Hands up!

Impalo and his car were surrounded by all these men in

plain clothes, guns drawn at him.

One of the men flashed his badge.

- Scotland Yard. Lay on the car! Face down!

They handcuffed and arrested him before he could get an inkling of what was going on. He was subjected to a speedy, expert search on his person. The policeman in civilian clothes was holding Impalo's passport, which he took from his shirt pocket. Then, they allowed him to turn over.

- I can see you are a diplomat, sir. Care to explain what you're doing here?

Impalo caught a glimpse of the box and notices, from his new position, that its door had been broken into. A few more seconds, and he returned to his senses.

- Untie me! I demand that you release me this instant! I have diplomatic immunity, you cannot arrest me.

- We'll get to the bottom of what you're getting up to, using your diplomatic *immunity*! You'd better have a good, detailed explanation of your presence and actions here, at this airport.

'*They sound like they're not messing about*'.

In addition to their palpable determination, Impalo now saw, up close and personal, how strong those broad-shouldered policemen were.

- I've got nothing to say.

- Into the car, *Sir*.

Impalo got into the police car without a single word. They rushed him over, sirens wailing and three cars behind the entire way, straight to the police station at Piccadilly.

CHAPTER 22

The Scotland Yard arrested the four men, placed each in a separate police car and took them to the Piccadilly Central Detainment Facility, where they were placed in different cells. Every now and then, one senior police officer after another came over to have a look at the men who got the London police so hot and bothered. The chief of Scotland Yard called a press conference, during which his best interrogators began working on the suspects.

- He isn't talking. What a bastard. He hasn't uttered a sound in hours.

- We've only got ourselves to blame for that.

- What makes you say that?

- Who do you think taught the Israelis about the rule of law? Their legal rights? They *know* they do not have to incriminate themselves.

- What make you think they're Israelis?

- Well, first off, they're the only one capable of such an operation. Second, the good doctor is cooperating. Thirdly, the attorney from Israel has been waiting to see his client for two hours now. He's even threatening to go to court unless we allow him to meet his client "this instant".

- What about the third guy?

- He won't stop talking. Queen's English, mind you, about anything at all, except for the abduction.

- Did they ask him what was he doing in the box?

- They sure did, but according to *his* version, he has no idea. He claims they promised him a free flight to Africa, and eventually - he ended up inside the box.

- What a tall tale. And what about the doctor?

- Such a stroke of genius to bring in a Russian translator to talk to him. That opened him up emotionally. He's been spilling his guts ever since.

- Stroke of luck! Would you like me to resume interrogating the Frenchie?

- What's the point?

- Well, I truly think there isn't. This buck won't produce any milk… He just sat there, quiet as the grave, during the whole session. He never even flinched when I called him on the French passport he had. At some point, I completely lost it and shoved it in his face, along with his photo. He didn't move a muscle. Nevertheless, the look he gave me made it clear I had better watch out.

- What a pro!

- And what about the diplomat?

- He's going out of his mind. He produces a card attesting he is indeed a member the diplomatic corps at the embassy of Jeronti. When we contacted them, they denied all knowledge of him and even claimed they have nothing to do with him.

- What do you believe?

- They're lying. It remains to be seen how all this will unfold. In the meantime, we have no choice. Go and have the Frenchie meet with his Israeli lawyer.

- What room?

- Five.

- Is everything ready there?

- Yes, but don't get your hopes up. These guys are pros. They will not utter a word beyond what they mean. You'll see, they'll smile, all pearly white, fully aware they're on camera.

*

- So, Dudi, you managed to drag me all the way to London, eh?

- I've always told you that representing me means never a dull moment...

- And you've always proven yourself right. Look, there's a problem with me representing you in England: since you didn't know in advance that you'd require my representation here, I did not secure a license to practice law here. According to British laws, I can always see you in jail, seeing as you're my client, nevertheless, I cannot represent you in court. Don't worry though. I have already made contact with an English law firm that came to us highly recommended, so their star solicitor will represent all three of you in the framework of all the legal proceedings.

- You have my full confidence.

- I got a chance to have a word with your wife before I got on the plane. She sounded very concerned. She intends to come to London in a matter of a few days. You've got a good wife there.

- Thanks, I know that.

- One more thing: I don't mind if they're recording this. You do not have to worry about the cost. Everything has been taken care of.

- Like I said, I know I can count on you.

- So goodbye for now. I'll see you in court tomorrow.

The South of London Court of Peace has never been the focus of such fuss and hullabaloo. Dozens of reporters and TV crews huddled around the old entrance, fighting over what few vacant seats were left in the court room, where the arraignment hearing was to take place. The circumstances of the arrest of the four men were the source of great interest not only to the members of the press, but also to hordes of ordinary citizens, who, likewise, came to partake of the unfolding drama. The palpable tension in the courtroom was underscored by the rumors that circulated that the Mossad was somehow involved in the alleged operation. The upcoming hearing, they all hoped, would shed additional, damning, light on the exciting role Israel's intelligence services "surely" played. The Israeli attorneys who arrived at the hearing were greeted with numerous questions to that effect, forcing to deny any involvement on the part of Mossad, but their protestations were met with ridicule and shrugging disbelief.

The British police, for its part, took no chances. They really pulled out all the stops, sparing no manpower, assigning dozens of uniform and plainclothes agents to patrol the immediate area of the court. In addition, the police set up a checkpoint at the entrance to the courtroom, complete with security inspection. The few members of the general public that did succeed in getting in along with the dozens of members of the press were bitterly disappointed: the proceedings lasted no more than thirty seconds. The prisoners' English attorney announced they consent to the police's request to detain them for an additional period of fifteen days. The detainees were then taken by another exit to the police cars that awaited them, and they were taken to the holding cells at Scotland Yard.

*

Later that afternoon, Dudi's Israeli attorney paid him a visit.

- How are you?

- Doing great. The court here is a lot like the one back in Netanya.

- Yes, it's all the same. They'll continue interrogating you now.

- No, they already began. Believe me, the police are the same everywhere, the investigators are no different. What they don't know is that Dudi is the same no matter what country he happens to be in.

- Did you give them your version of events?

- Of course not. After all, it was you who taught me never to cooperate with the police, whichever form they take; good cop or bad cop. I kept my mouth shut, or, as you lawyers put it, "the right to remain silent".

- That's right. Still, I would tell the interrogators that what happened has nothing whatsoever to do with the State of Israel, and that Mossad had nothing do with it either. That's the main thing.

- Roger that. I'll tell them.

Dudi's attorney went to visit him again two weeks later.

- When I got back to Israel, I received a call from someone who asked to see me concerning your case. I told him I wasn't interested in any meeting. I can't tell whether he was offended or not. He didn't sound hurt by my reply. He asked me to tell you two things: first, that you mustn't get him wrong, and second, that he would take care of your family and the rest, that everyone's family will receive financial support for as long as you're all under arrest.

- Let me tell you two things: first, I know who the person

who called you is; second, I am not wrong about him, and third, do not get between myself and that person.

- Gotcha. Now listen, I've met with your English lawyers. They're expecting your indictment within two weeks from now.

- That's good news. In any case, it's better to be a prisoner than a detainee. So I'll see you when my trial begins. Ah, before I forget: I saw my wife and she told me how well you've been taking care of her. Thank you.

*

The indictment against the four men was issued two weeks after that meeting between Dudi and his attorney. The four were accused of abduction. Dudi met with his lawyer again right after the indictment hearing.

- The first hearing, at which the prosecution will level its case against you, is scheduled for one month from now. Until then, we have to agree on our line of defense and prepare accordingly. The English solicitors are of the opinion the battle should be fought over the penalty rather than the actual conviction. What's your opinion, Dudi?

- What's yours?

- I think they're right. You cannot argue that you "just happened to be there", that you 'saw this box' and that you "got in there by mistake".

- Doing time gives me time to think, you know. Just remember all those times, dozens of cases, when I was arrested and arraigned but was never actually convicted. And you know why that is?

- Why?

- Because I never pleaded guilty. I think I've showed you my list of principles once. Never pleading guilty is right at the top.

- So what shall we argue, then? That you were framed? That they kidnapped you too? Don't forget this is an English court of law, where they have no sense of humor. They don't even need anyone to turn state evidence in order to convict you.

- So what do you propose?

- That you adopt a more flexible approach to your principles. You and your friends are clearly going away for quite a few years. Our struggle is about for how long. Our focus should be on the sentence. We cannot plead your innocence. You have no recourse but to plead guilty.

- I don't mind doing time. Prison doesn't scare me one bit. The question is whether this is the only option.

- Your English solicitors are pros. They know the law inside out, as well as the mentality of the local court system, which, as you know, is no less important.

- Yes, they are fine men.

- I spent hours debating the case with them, and we all came to the conclusion you have no other option but to admit your guilt. English courts can be very appreciative of defendants who plead guilty rather than drag the whole thing. Another point is in our favor as well: the whole story about the kidnapping has had enormous coverage in the press, which is something the English aren't used to, or anyone else, come to think of it. This entire business has struck a chord of romance and adventure, helped by the fact this scandal involves foreigners, that England just happened to be the venue, that no Englishman was hurt, no British interests were undermined.

- What are you trying to say?

- That if you were to plead guilty to the charges, and I

see no other option, we would be providing the court with considerations to go easy on you, rather than face a twenty-year sentence, which is what the law stipulates.

- So how do we make this happen?

- We plead guilty when the prosecution makes its case and calls us out on the facts. Then, we make our own case for leniency.

- So, like you said, I need to be flexible about my own principles. But I'll have you know, this will not happen again. Very well then. Go for it. Let's hope for the best.

*

Scores of reporters and spectators filled the courtroom at the South London District Court. They all came to hear the verdict in " Crown vs. Kidnappers", as the press called it. The public never tire of the story, so the papers and TV never cease to fan the flames, forever covering it in the crime section. The men pleaded guilty in an earlier hearing, so the judges' verdict was all that's left. They began their decision by recounting the chain of events, after which they referred to each of the accused in detail.

In the matter of Eli, the judges determined he headed the operation and was the primary perpetrator. An Israeli national who had arrived in London under a false passport from Jeronti, it was he who recruited Dudi and the doctor to the affair. The justices did accept Eli's claims that he took it upon himself to organize the abduction believing he was acting on some patriotic sense of duty, guided by his understanding he was somehow serving the interests of the State of Israel by cultivating its ties with Jeronti. The court even accepted Eli's claims he was convinced they were abducting a criminal, a convicted felon whose own country had convicted him of serious counts of fraud and corruption, and whose repatriation and subsequent incarceration would be a great service to the rule of law. The justices further uploaded Eli's admission of complicity and guilt in the kidnapping, thereby saving the legal system substantial time and expense. In their verdict, the judges noted that without making light of the gravity of the perpetrators' actions, they were nevertheless unarmed, attesting to their clear and deliberate intentions never to harm the kidnapped in any way, nor anyone else. The justices further credited Eli with the fact that in the framework of his preparations ahead of the operation, he took it upon himself to purchase medical supplies and safety measures in order to ensure Biko's well-being and to prevent any danger to his life. The court further stipulated unequivocally, that this was a criminal action rather than a terrorist act. In their final clause, the judges sentenced Eli to fourteen years in prison.

As for the doctor, the court determined that for the matter of actual sentencing, they must take into consideration his guilty plea, despite the fact he had no other recourse. The judges further stipulated that per numerous testimonies from Israel, the defendant was of good and solid character, that he had saved the lives of numerous men and women, and that he was a highly capable professional. The justices accepted the defendant's admission as well as his explanation that he was entirely convinced the abduction was carried out in the framework of some coordination with Israel Intelligence Community. The court noted the doctor's gratitude to the State of Israel and his sense of patriotic duty to repay his adoptive country for its kindness in affording him refuge, gainful employment and a social status, having fled the Soviet Union under dire circumstances. The judges also attributed much to the doctor's great care for his patient, the abducted person under his care, as well as his insistence the box be fitted with any conceivable means to secure Biko's health and safety, pursuant to the doctor's persistent demands that he be equipped with all the medical equipment required to keep his patient in the best condition possible.

The justices emphasized in particular, the doctor's complete compliance, immediately upon his apprehension and arrest, and his voluntary disclosure of all the medical information the British doctors required to maintain Biko's health post the latter's sedation, including but not exclusively the exact dosage of sedatives used. This precise data concerning the injection and so forth allowed the doctors assigned to Biko to monitor his condition, offer him the best possible course of treatment and revive him effectively. The judges also noted, non sequitur, that the kidnapped remained in a coma for an additional eight hours after he was taken to hospital. In conclusion, the verdict was ten year sentence.

With regard to Dudi, the court determined that he played a merely secondary role in the whole affair, having been dragged into it by Eli, his longtime friend. In relation to this finding, the judges noted that Dudi was a man whose weak, easy going and suggestible nature caused him to be taken in all too easily and that he was susceptible to untoward influence. The court also referred to numerous character references in Dudi's favor, attesting to his charitable nature and countless good deeds. The judges ended their verdict by sentencing Dudi to ten years in prison.

The fourth and final accused was Benino Impalo, whose

plea for diplomatic immunity the court rejected forthwith, claiming it does not hold in the case of a crime having been committed. The justices further determined that the officer was in charge of all the arrangements in the framework of the kidnapping, including the contact with the airplane. They therefore denied the defendant's claims he was merely following orders as he was bound to, being a soldier. They did not accept his assertion that he behaved "as expected of a man in uniform who had taken an oath of obedience," and sentenced him to twelve years.

After sentencing, the convicted men were summarily taken to London's main prison ahead of being sent to serve their respective sentences in different jails. They were no longer detainees but rather convicted men soon to become prisoners, "Her Majesty's guests". At the end of processing, each was indeed sent to a different penitentiary in the UK.

It was decided that Dudi be sent to serve out his sentence in the South London Maximum Facility, so the following day, he was taken there by police car. After a short process of registration and so on, he was taken, cuffed arms and feet, through numerous steel doors and rattling keys, to cell 38, at the far end of one of the prison wards. One of the three jailors taking him there pulled out this huge key and unlocked the steel door to the cell, unchained Dudi's hands and legs and pushed him in.

The cell was designed to accommodate four inmates. It had a concrete floor and a single high window, way up, with bars. One of the corners served as an open lavatory, without any walls, and the two bunk beds were bolted to the floor. The three inmates who received Dudi all wore striped prison uniforms.

- We heard you were Jewish, let's see.

Dudi recalled his own principles. The second, to never seek anyone else's protection, and the fifth: Once you're inside, be sure to establish your standing immediately. Never let them walk all over you.' Boldly and coldly, he looked his fellow cell mates straight in the face, silently warning them to stay the h*ll away.

- Do as ya' told, you c*nt!

The three prisoners approached him menacingly. Within a split second, Dudi hammered his head against one of them, blowing him across the cell. He kicked the other in the groin, rendering him reeling on the nearby bed. As for the third, he received yet another kick, which broke his ribs, sending him tumbling to the floor of the lavatory. Secure in his position, having rendered them completely unconscious, Dudi proceeded to arrange his few belongings on the vacant bed.

The cell door flung open and in walked a large team of jailors, who couldn't be more amazed to find, waiting for them, the most gruesome scene of three men, out cold and writhing with pain. They were undoubtedly expecting to find the new inmate tending to his wounds, having been left to the devices of his fellow cell members, but this wasn't the case. A medical team quickly arrived at the scene and took the three aching bullies away.

Dudi, for his part, was placed in solitary confinement that very day, as decreed by the prison's warden, for a period of no less than seven days. His cell was scarcely bigger than five feet by seven, which was hardly enough to stretch one's limbs. The corner of his new cell featured a lavatory that was so narrow, he had to stand up in order to relieve himself. The tiny cell's large steel door would open only three times a day, in order to shove his bowl of food in. 'Still way more comfortable than that box,' he smiled to himself as he lay on his narrow bed, calm and serene, reciting his own ten principles.

- I heard they made you king of your prison!
- Where d'ya hear that?
- That's what they've told me when I showed them my pass as your attorney.
- Well, a good reputation is all that matters these days.
- How did you pull that off?
- I merely adhered to my own principles. Look up sections two and five, would you.
- I'll be sure to do just that. You always were a man of mystery. So what are we going to do now? Ten years is more than we bargained for.
- No fear. We'll appeal.
- Dudi, you know the chances are slim. The appellate court rarely overturns verdicts.
- I know. But I also know that "*the righteous person will live by his faithfulness*" (Habakkuk 2:4).

*

Wearing his official colorful garments and carrying a decorated staff with a silver ball, the bailiff entered the main courtroom at the Old Bailey, Central Criminal Court of England and Wales. He then proceeded to beat three times and declared "Order in court!"

The four appellants rose from their seats on the right side of the corner, along with their assigned guards from the London police. The crown's counselors, headed by the district prosecutor got up in the front row, on the other side of which stood the defendants' solicitors. The crowd, comprising the press and more curious members of the general public also rose to their feet, as befitting the senior circuit of England's and indeed the world's most famous court of appeals. The three judges, headed by Lord Justice Johnson, took their red seats facing the courtroom.

- Please be seated!

Dudi watched the crown's magistrates with amusement. He has a great deal of experience with judges, dating back to his protracted imprisonment in the framework of his trial as a defendant in a murder case. He even argued before Israel's Supreme Court in the framework of his own motion against the practice of tying peoples' legs when brought before the court for arraignment. This was such an important appeal, five Israeli Supreme Court justices sat for this panel, which the court eventually granted, ruling there was no cause to continue with that means. They even praised Dudi for his eloquence and dignified appearance. '*Still, none of my judges over the years ever had a wig on like these three,*' he couldn't help thinking. '*Nevertheless, I have no false hopes about their upcoming verdict.*' He passed the time trying to imagine Justice of the Peace Bergersson from Netanya wearing a hairpiece.

The head of the panel, Lord Justice Johnson, began reading out the verdict, cutting Dudi's musings short:

- In the case of Crown vs Eli et al., the court finds...

But Dudi had already reached the conclusion Justice Bergersson was nicer looking without a wig.

Either way, the verdict at the Old Bailey was a foregone conclusion: the esteemed court rejected their appeal against their penalty, reaffirming the reasons proffered by the lower court that had ruled before. The Old Bailey panel further noted they were presented with no evidence to suggest that either the State of Israel or Jeronti were in any way shape or form connected with the abduction operation. The judges concurred with their predecessors from the district court as to the complicity of all four men in a "private undertaking". The panel of three Old Bailey justices refused to refer to Bwana Biko's actions, as laid out by the counselors from the defense, ruling they were neither capable nor in any need to establish, let alone determine, whether Biko was indeed guilty of the charges the defense team leveled at him.

"In any case," the court concluded, "the means the defendants adopted in order to deliver Biko to justice is not in line with the norms, and they are duly proscribed by the rule of law."

"Order in courtroom!"

Every person in the gallery joined the member of the legal profession in rising to their feet, seeing the justices off. Four separate cars took each of the prisoners back to his respective prison.

PART THREE

CHAPTER 23

- Hello, who is this?

- This is Assaf Shlomi. I would like to speak with Chief of Staff Mkume Shibu. It's urgent. He knows me.

- Please hold.

Assaf was kept on hold for quite a few moments before he was told:

- I was asked to tell you the chief of staff isn't in today. Goodbye.

A few hours later, Assaf called again. This time, he used the private number Shibu had given him in better, bygone, days.

- This is Assaf Shlomi again. I hope Mkume Shibu is back. I'd like to speak with him urgently.

- I am sorry. They've asked me to tell you the chief of staff won't be coming today at all.

- I would like to leave my number. Miss, please have him call me as soon as possible. I have an important message to convey to him.

- Thank you, sir, but there is no point leaving a phone number. The chief of staff is not in the habit of returning phone calls. Besides, I really must get back, there are many calls waiting. Thank you.

*

The very next day, Assaf dialed the secret number he had once again. It was disconnected. That very day, he took the British Airways flight to London, where he boarded the next flight to Golasa. During his flight, he wondered whether it would have made better sense to advise Shibu's office he was coming there and save the terrible traffic to the capital, let alone the line at passports and customs.

The line was indeed unbearable. The station for persons with foreign passports was shut, so hundreds of passengers had to contend with two stalls. It was a multitude of colorful jellabiyas and tailored business suits, women with multi-colored turbans huddled together, babies crying and children shouting and all. The strong scent of spices and body odor dominated the air, underscored by the ineffective ACs, if they were even working. After a very long time, Assaf finally reached the stand, all sweaty. He handed the officer his British passport. As he was accustomed to doing, he haphazardly looked out of the terminal, looking for the Mercedes with the chauffer. But the counter clerk in front of him was behaving differently now. He wasn't sluggish anymore, but rather excited and visibly concerned, as attested to by his sweaty brow. His lips were quivering and Assaf could tell the man's hand was looking for a button under the desk. The people in the line behind grumbled at the sight of the delay, but the agent didn't flinch. Soon came two tall men in dark suits and relieved the passport stand clerk of his unwelcome guest. They asked Assaf to accompany them.

- Do you have any extra luggage?

They looked at his carry-on bag. Assaf shook his head, so

they took him to the British Airways stand.

- The flight to London is leaving in half an hour. Kindly board it.

Assaf wouldn't have it. He rallied:

- But I have an appointment at with the president's chief of staff!

- The flight to London is about to leave. We strongly suggest you do not miss it.

Assaf realized they were determined and that there was no other recourse. The attendant at British Airways demanded he pay for changing the return flight to that same date. He didn't argue and handed her his credit card, booked a coach seat and allowed the two burly men to take him right to the plane. As they cleared him back through passports and customs.

The moment Assaf stepped inside the plane, one of the men told him:

- We were asked to tell you never to return to Jeronti.

Assaf look out the window and saw them. They were still there when the plane took off.

*

Assaf was no quitter. As soon as he returned to Israel, he made his own inquiry and discovered Jomo, one of his own students back at the Intelligence school for foreign agents. He followed up and learned that Jomo was now serving at Jeronti's embassy in Rome and holding a key position there. So Assaf looked for the next flight to Rome and landed there a few hours later. Upon entering the embassy, he saw a security guard.

- Hi, I am Assaf Shlomi. Would do me a favor, please? Can you tell Jomo that Assaf from the course is here and wishing to see him?

Jomo came down within seconds. He hugged Assaf warmly and invited him back into his office.

- I've always looked up to you, you know. I am so glad you're here. How did you find me? What can I do for you?

- Well, you know I have no problem locating old friends. All I'm asking is that you pass a message along in my name.

- What's the message and to whom shall I pass it on?

- It concerns a mutual friend of ours, the President Chief of Staff Mkume Shibu.

- What do you need me for? After all, he's one of your biggest fans!

- Something has gone wrong recently, so I need to deliver him an urgent message. Vital Jeronti interests are at stake.

His host's face immediately fell. His palpable concern now replaced his earlier joy and enthusiasm.

- I hope you're not getting me in some trouble.

- I would never do that to my friends. What I am asking from you is only for the best of Jeronti.

- What you are asking me to do?

- Please tell Mkume Shibu that for the benefit of Jeronti, as well as for his own sake, he had better meet me as soon as possible.

- Is that your entire message?

- Yes. He knows how to get hold of me. I am ready to see him at any time and place of his own choosing.

Looking ever so glum, Jomo accompanied Assaf to the gate.

*

Several days later Assaf received a call from an unlisted

number. He immediately understood Jomo was on the line from Rome:

- It's me, Jomo. Please come to the embassy this Tuesday at eleven o'clock.

Assaf showed up on time. Expecting his arrival, the embassy's securi guard showed him to a room at the end of a long corridor.

- You asked to see me.

Shibu was wearing a business suit. Assaf began.

- You could have saved me the journey to Rome, as well as the time of the security man outside the door, if only you were willing to see me back in Jeronti.

Grim faced, he answered Assaf.

- This isn't the Mossad here. You don't tell me what to do. What's this all about?

- You're right, of course. Nevertheless, back at the Mossad, we would have done a better job hiding the cameras, as well as placing the recording device in plain sight. It gives your guests a better feeling.

Mkume Shibu smiled ever so briefly.

- I did tell them I had a special guest, so they need to do a special job. Okay. What's on your mind?

- It's simple. I am still expecting my ten million. I want them soon, thank you.

- What are you talking about?

- Getting paid for a job well done! Remember the first thing I taught you at the introductory training course, all those years ago: "an intelligence operative is bound by honor. Promises made must be kept".

- And I remember my introductory lecture in the course on economics I took at Oxford. The first they taught us was what the term "return" means: "no goods, no money".

- But you must have missed the course on word-keeping. I *delivered* the *goods*. The client was right there in the box, waiting just for you.

- We received no goods. On top of that, we lost face on your account.

- Look, stop being clever. It was you people who messed up. You failed to keep your end of our bargain. You're the only reason Biko never reached Jeronti. I expect to be paid what you owe me. In full.

- Are you threatening me?

- Not in the least. I am merely explaining myself.

- We've already discussed the whole issue of payment. President Imru called a meeting, following which he determined you are not entitled to any additional payment. It is only thanks to our friendship that we'll forgo the return of the down payment you were given. Consider yourself lucky. One million dollars is a great deal of money.

- Kindly tell your president he is wrong. I'm not to be trifled with. You mistake me for someone who backs down. I will not give up on one red cent that is due me. Like I said, no threats, just a clarification: you people are in deep. Do not make it worse.

- What do you mean?

- The fact that you were somehow successful in convincing powers that be that the whole abduction was "a private undertaking" will not help you. Three men, the president, yourself, and I, know the truth, and whose idea this was. You lot know all too well the kind of damage Jeronti would face in case the actual facts came out. You may tell your president that at the very least, the fallout from the publication would mean that he can forget about ever visiting London. He might sooner come before The International Court of Justice at The Hague.

- I'll pass that on to President Imru.

- Before I go, I would like to tell you one other thing. If you get up to any ideas, forget about it. All it takes has already been recorded, both on tape and on film. If anything should happen to me, a vault would burst open, and its entire contents shall be unleashed to the world.

Assaf's phone rang again with the unknown number about a week later:

- It's me, Jomo. Long time no see. I'd love to see you. Next Tuesday at eleven o'clock, please.

'Talk about Déjà vu: same security guard. Same corridor,' Assaf thought.

Then, at Jomo's office, he greeted Assaf smiling. His face was beaming.

- We highly appreciate you, Assaf. We know you're a man of honor. Then again, these things take time, you know. They've asked me to have you sign these forms, please. It's a secret waiver. Thanks. Now, what's your bank account number, please?

- Here. I don't need to read before I sign. I trust you people.

After he signed and exchanged a few more pleasantries, the embassy car returned Assaf to the airport.

CHAPTER 24

Very few residents on the moshav, the small farming community where Assaf had grown up, had continued to pursue with agriculture over the years. One of them was his father. He had his own orange grove, dating back to his own father, Assaf's grandfather, who started it in the 1940s. This orchard wasn't merely a source of income, but also the focal point of their entire family. Each and every event and memory were tied to it, from joyous and happy occasions, all sorts of experiences, to sad times and vexing events. Assaf's parents wed there, celebrated his bar mitzvah, and marked his grandfather's passing by holding a memorial event there before burying him at the local cemetery.

Assaf took to visiting his father at the orange grove. They used to have cheese sandwiches for lunch by the concrete reservoir, on the higher side of their land, sharing olives and sliced vegetables. The pool was empty during the summer, but it filled each winter with the rain, when, as if out of nowhere, green toads would appear, filling the whole orchard with their sounds and offspring.

"My father built this pool in those days," his father told him once, on one of Assaf's first visits. "This used to be the source of irrigation for the entire grove. See that concrete top there, by the side? This was the mouth of the well. My father dug it all by himself, using nothing but a shovel and hoe. He drove the water up using a pump, which delivered the water to the trees."

- How did the water get to the trees?

- My father dug a cement canal which branched out along and across the entire orchard. Every now and then, they diverted the water to a different ditch. Each tree had its own moat and waterway. When I used to help out in the summers, he had a special role for me: I had to block the flow using this barrier. I would remove a sack filled with dirt, let the water run, fill the moat and then stop the current again, move on to the next tree and so on. My dad used to be so proud of me.

Assaf kept imagining his grandfather, whom he remembered as this huge man with smiling blue eyes, following his son, Assaf's own father, with his eyes as he removed those water barriers. The family drew its pride and livelihood from the orchard, but mostly pride. It's not that they wanted for anything, but they could not afford any luxury or indulge themselves. They got used to living frugally. Assaf had to hitch a ride to the beach to see Dudi. He couldn't afford the bus fare. His friend, Hagay, had his own horse. He didn't even dream about owning a horse.

Assaf's parents paid for admission to a military boarding school by cutting down on their own expenses, which were already minimal, as well as through loans from relatives. As a cadet and as a soldier, Assaf had virtually no income, or very little pay to speak of. He had to make do with the pocket money his folks gave him on extremely rare occasions, which helped him make ends meet.

However high his salary from the Mossad, it barely covered his expenses, since by then he was married and supporting his wife through her architecture studies at Israel's Technion, Israel Institute of Technology. Seeing as rent and living expenses gobbled up pretty much every hard earned penny, he was forced to ask for a loan against his next salary almost each month.

Suddenly, Assaf had ten million dollars to his name! Actually, it was "only" nine million. He kept the advance he received in the form of the first million dollars in a special bank account in Israel, which he used to fund the expenses that the operation incurred. Once Assaf's four mates were sentenced back in London, he told them he would extend to each of their families - excluding Benino Impalo, of course - two thousand dollars each month for the duration of their incarceration. His three friends' families were indeed taken care of. The same account proved deep enough to finance all legal expenses too, easily covering their defense - with enough to spare out of that one million.

But that was as far as his generosity went. *'Jeronti's government's debt to the Israeli team was hereby settled once the one million dollars were paid off. That much is clear,'* he figured. He also made it abundantly clear to his friends through the attorney he paid for: "Jeronti's government never got its money's worth. No goods: no cash!" That's what he had them tell Dudi, Eli, and the good doctor.

Nevertheless, *'any additional funds I receive from Jeronti is mine, and mine alone, a personal debt their government owes Me,'* he justified himself resolutely. *'Time I took care of myself, and myself only,'* Assaf vowed.

CHAPTER 25

A row of magnolia trees greeted Dudi along his walk to the manor house. He relished the mild scent that dominated the air, mixing with the smell of fresh cut grass. The huge mansion was made entirely of wood. Built on raised grounds, it dominated the entire land and its surroundings. On the right hand side of the house, among the trees, stood this elongated wooden hut, with stables to boot. Dudi spotted a man in work boots and a wide brim straw hat forking hay to three beautiful horses: one white, one black, and one brown. To the left of the manor's driveway, he saw a patch of roses. Their bloom was stunning. This was spring incarnate. *'Such a far cry from my jail back in London,'* Dudi mused.

As he entered, he was greeted by an Asian woman who led him through a spacious living room, albeit simply furnished, to this huge porch that overlooked the manor's lovely view.

- I've been waiting for you!

There was Assaf, seated on this wide armchair complete with multi-colored cushions. He was wearing a white tracksuit. When he saw Dudi, he rose from his seat to hug him, but Dudi repelled Assaf gently but forcefully nonetheless.

- You look great! I knew you'd get along just fine.

- Cut the bullshit!

'He must've picked up that English accent in jail,' Assaf couldn't help wondering to himself.

- I'm not here for compliments.

Assaf didn't move a muscle. His face remained frozen, as did his azure eyes, once the coveted prize of all the girls in the neighborhood.

- So why have you come?

- To settle the score.

Dudi never raised his voice. His face imbued power, his piercing eyes and the impressive figure he cut were enough to instill the proper air with any viewer. Even at that moment, after his long and difficult flight, he still looked like he had just been to a hair salon. He must have picked up a brand new white designer shirt and tailored pants.

- I have no idea what you're talking about.

Assaf's had let his long blond hair grow even longer since Dudi last saw him.

'His cheek bones and full lips are the same as they always were,' Dudi thought, recalling how impressive his friend always looked, attracting everyone who saw him, from those girls at the beach way back when to all those intelligence agents, down to the last operative under Assaf's command.

- Oh, I am sure you do. You had seven years to prepare.

The blue eyes and the brown eyes locked, gazing at one another, judging the other's resolve, waiting to see who would cave first.

- What *score* are you talking about, Dudi? For seven years straight, I made sure your wife gets her monthly support. I also covered all your legal expenses.

- I'm not talking about small change.

- What are you talking about, then?

- The payment we were promised for the operation, as well as compensation for all those years behind bars.

- We? Who's *we*?

- Unlike some people I know, I do not abandon my friends.

- Neither do I. I'm still your friend. I feel the same as I did back when we used to surf the waves.

- You're no friend. I did time because of you, so did Eli and the doc. You let us rot in jail all those years while you were living it up at our expense.

- Why would you say such a thing? Why is it my fault?

- Seven years I've been waiting to tell you what I think of you to your face, and seven years I have been waiting to get what's coming to me. It isn't about the money as much as it's the principle of the matter.

- But what did I do wrong?

The Asian maid appeared at the doorstep of the living room.

- May I offer you something to drink?

- The guest would like to have a glass of water. As for me, please bring me my usual.

- Let me remind you, then. Last time we met, you took it upon yourself, you gave me your word that everything was done, all loose ends tied and that there will be no hitch when it comes to the things you were responsible for. The entire operation went south because of you. It's time for you to get what's coming to you.

Assaf's maid returned with the glass of water for Dudi and whisky on the rocks for Assaf and disappeared.

- I have no idea what you're talking about!

- Seven years, day after day, night after night, I kept wondering to myself, 'why didn't Assaf join us there? Why did he stay away?' For seven years, every night, I kept thinking 'oh boy, that mofo just left us in jail, he's having the time of his life at our expense.' Where's our money?

- What money?

- Just quit it, would you? This isn't the Mossad. You pulled it off there, but you will not get away with it with me! You sent people to their death at Isfahan while you stayed behind. You sent us on a dangerous operation too and kept your distance. We aren't like those people that you've abandoned. I know everything about the operation at Isfahan, and just like that, I also know everything about the money!

- Dudi, I am asking you again, what money?

- All of it. Your share too. It's only fair, compensation for everything you put us through.

Years of interrogating suspects, running agents and engaging in psychological warfare were at stake, but still, Assaf's opponent was a far cry from those he had encountered during his career. At the Mossad, he often regretted he didn't have someone like Dudi by his side. From time to time, when faced with a real operational dilemma, he would often wonder how Dudi would have acted. But now, not only was Dudi not there for him, he was against him, a staunch adversary, armed with first rate self-control, cunning and clever, with ice running through his veins.

Assaf knew he couldn't allow himself to fail.

- The money they gave me up front, I spent on your family and the others', as well as on legal fees.

Assaf had his game face on. Blood, bold and resolute, he indeed imbued power and confidence.

- You're still at it. Stop trying to trick me. I ain't buying this s**t. I know everything. The inquest after Isfahan got you off scot free because they wanted to extricate themselves as much as you. But this is different, this time it's just you, me, and the truth.

- I didn't receive any money except for the advance they gave me.

So you wanna tell me all this is from your pension from the Mossad?

Dudi continued sardonically. He never once raised his voice when he added:

- Remember, Dudi is not one to be trifled with, or betrayed. No one ever cheats me!

He got up without another word, crossed the living room, thanked Assaf's Asian maid graciously and warmly, went along the driveway and climbed into his rented car, which he had parked near the mansion's gate.

CHAPTER 26

Boaz Harari showed up early at the café. A tall man, albeit bent, he had few remaining hairs and many lines across his face. He sat at a corner table and without waiting for Assaf, ordered a coffee with soy milk and a croissant. He helped himself to a newspaper from the stand and took in the peaceful morning. He loved frequenting that particular coffee shop, primarily because of its rustic atmosphere, complete with a terrace overlooking orchards, groves and green fields. He also liked the fact that the tables were rather remote from one another. Boaz sat on this well-cushioned country-style armchair that wasn't hard for his back, which began aching of late. Only after he finished all the newspapers as well as his coffee, did Assaf appear and take the armchair across from Boaz.

- Thank you for agreeing to see me here in the countryside. You know I'd be happy to meet up any place of your choosing.

- It was my choosing. I like it here. It's my favorite spot, and it has a good effect on me. My back begins to ache the moment I start thinking about those narrow wooden chairs in all those cafés near the police headquarters.

- I always knew how spoiled you lot are, but I never thought the police has the time to sit at coffee shops.

- Just kidding. We are always busy, but I'll have time for

cafés soon enough.

- What happened? The commissioner finally decided to give you the boot?

Boaz, a highly decorated chief in police intelligence for many years, smiled albeit faintly.

- Even old boys like me get tired. I shall retire at the end of this year. I'll be a pensioner.

- Boaz the *pensioner*? It doesn't sound right to me. I can already imagine the parties all the murderers are going to throw, along with all those rapists, corrupt thieves, robbers and the rest of Israel's 'finest'.

- Don't worry. The country will do just fine without me. I already have replacements lined up. They'll do as well as I did. But before we move on to business, you have to hear this latest joke. There was this mouse, you see. He didn't feel too well-

'*Here we go again,*' Assaf thought to himself.

Boaz was infamous for his obsessive joke-telling. He would always force his listeners to hear "the latest joke" at the beginning of any meeting or operation, citing that "laughter frees up the mind, gets the creative juices flowing", or so he would tell his almost literally captive audience.

- So when the mouse left work early one day, on account of not feeling well, he got home, only to find his wife, Mrs. Mouse, 'in flagrante', doing the deed with a bat. "You cheater," cried the mouse, "how could you cheat on me with such an ugly creature?" So Mrs. Mouse tells him, do you hear? "Sure he's ugly, but at least he can fly…"

Boaz Harari was considered by all, from his subordinates through to his friends to his superiors, a "walking computer". He began his career in the police as a mere policeman with his own neighborhood patrol, moved on to the district intelligence branch and was then promoted to the national intelligence branch at HQ. His memory was no less than phenomenal. They would often say of him, that no "serious" criminal in Israel was unfamiliar to Boaz. He was also highly admired for his proven ability to make the most accurate predictions and come up with the uncanny insights concerning the criminal world. His intelligence reports and briefs were regularly downloaded by the top echelons, seeing as they allowed the various operational forces to study events from the criminals' own perspective, thereby assisting in solving numerous cases - not to mention preventing quite a few too. He embodied tenacity, staunch resolve and sticking to one's guns until the case is cracked.

Police academies in Israel used to have the cadets study the case of one Nachman Levi, a criminal who had disappeared without a trace some twelve years earlier. The police force is not in the habit of closing cases of this kind. Nevertheless, the passage of time, the lack of any clues and the investigators' preference for more pressing cases, coupled with their lack of enthusiasm to deal with a "cold case", all resulted in this person's fate being pushed further and further down the pile. Boaz came across it quite randomly, and he soon realized there's a great deal more to it than merely a missing person's case. He therefore began pursuing it, turning over stone after stone, following any shred of evidence, however faint, and constantly going against the grain in search of new leads. Eventually, Boaz apprised the chiefs of intelligence and operations of his investigation and told them about a remote dune somewhere at the beach in Bat Yam, south of Tel Aviv. The police spent two days searching there, and indeed found the remains of Nachman's body. Thanks to this discovery, not only could the deceased's family finally lay him to rest, but the police uncovered further evidence that helped unravel a criminal organization that was a scourge on the entire country.

- So what are your plans for retirement? I heard you like horses, so you'd better know I am on the lookout for someone to handle my steeds. The pay isn't all that high, but you are guaranteed satisfaction.

- Thanks. Did you really call me to offer me a job?

- The job is yours. But before that, I would like to pick your brain about a personal matter.

- Dudi Dayan.

- How did you know?

- Yesterday at four past four in the afternoon, an El Al plane landed here at Ben Gurion after taking off from Vienna. Dudi goes through border and customs. He rents a car at four forty-two and arrives at your mansion at half past five. Pretty good, considering the traffic. He leaves at ten to six, which took me by surprise, since I thought you two would have a lot of catching up to do, having last laid eyes on one another seven years earlier. Dudi gets home twenty minutes after leaving your place. I knew you'd be calling. I even canceled a meeting scheduled for this morning.

- I'm beginning to think you also know what he and I talked about.

- No, I do not. We're not allowed to listen in without a court order. Besides, we're merely following up on our case.

- You're an old and trusted friend of mine. We go back many years. I'd like to consult with you on the matter of Dudi.

Boaz was indeed a longtime acquaintance of Assaf's. They had often shared data as colleagues from the police and Mossad, respectively. Both organizations had many mutual interests, primarily when it came to internal affairs, usually the purview of the police, as well as numerous operations worldwide, so it was only natural for them both to cooperate and bond over background material they supplied one another, such persons of interests, alibi and coverage the police provided Mossad operatives and so on. Their professional cooperation evolved into a friendship, fueled by their mutual appreciation for each other.

Assaf invoked Dudi's name without any sign of excitement. Boaz noted that nothing about the demeanor of his friend and colleague attested to any form of distress: his face remained frozen and his voice was mild. Nevertheless, Boaz did notice Assaf's sweat, which could only spell one thing. Boaz's experience had taught him that perspiration often, if not always, is something no one can control, unlike one's muscles, facial expressions and body language. One lesson from his many thousands of hours interrogating people was that sweat meant pressure. Stress. Boaz realized that Assaf's sweaty brow was a tell-tale sign.

- Did something happen yesterday? I thought this was merely a reunion of two friends who hadn't seen each other for many years.

- It's true. Dudi and I last saw each other seven years ago, but this was no friendly reunion.

- So what was it about, this meeting that got you so worked up?

- Dudi asked me for money.

Boaz showed no sign of surprise. He looked at Assaf for a long time, noticing his perspiration intensifying.

- Do you owe Dudi any money?

- That's what he claims. But I would rather refrain from answering you directly. I asked you to see me since you're an expert on all matters concerning Dudi, so that you might advise me how to handle him.

- Assaf, look, we've known each other for many years now, and as much as I appreciate your unwillingness to answer me directly, we both know I am still on duty. I am entrusted with the law. Even among friends. You don't always have to say everything, but I then again, I believe you know Dudi better than me, so you know better than me how to conduct yourself with him.

- I've known Dudi since I was ten. We've always been as close as can be. We've gone through so much together, not to mention London.

- Don't tell me about that. Believe me, I know all the details of the abduction operation.

- You do not know *all* the details. Best we keep it that way.

- Oh, don't start that all over again, your old 'who knows more' routine. Believe me when I tell you I know everything there is to know, except for the contents of your conversation yesterday.

- I met a different Dudi yesterday. Something happened to him in jail back in London. You're right, I did think I knew him better than I know my own self, but that was true until yesterday. The Dudi I saw at home yesterday was not the Dudi I know. Actually, what I came across made me anxious, so I called you up for your opinion.

- Did he threaten you? Would you like to involve the police? They've had some rest from him, for seven years, but as you see, he's on top of the list. They haven't lost sight of him, not for one moment.

- No. He didn't make any threats. He didn't have to. Nevertheless, as you can tell, he did get his message across. I didn't ask for this meeting in order to press charges against him. I also don't think there's any point. You guys failed when it comes to Dudi. You of all people know he has never been convicted. Not even once.

- So what is it that you want from me?

- I am here to consult an old friend. Tell me what to do.

- I won't ask you again whether you owe him any money, but I do want to tell you that Dudi has his own moral standards. In the entire catalog of files we have on him, there is not a single record of him giving anyone a hard time for no reason but beware he who tricks him or owes him any money.

Assaf's face hardened. During his entire tenure at the Mossad, he gained a reputation as someone who couldn't be threatened and as a person addicted to challenge and adversity. Mention the words 'real tough' to him, and he's invigorated, not just motivated. The moment Assaf makes up his mind, he would let no one, let alone someone from the other side of the tracks, siphon off his hard earned money.

Assaf recalled his last conversation with Mkume Shibu. '*He was right. We did work on the basis of success. Having failed to deliver the goods, never mind for what reason, they were not entitled to any payment. Even the money we did receive upfront was a gesture of good will. The boys ought to be grateful we weren't asked to give it back. The nine million I got in person is mine. I have no intention of sharing that with anyone*'.

Boaz could see Assaf wasn't sweating anymore.

- It's getting late. Gotta go. Please don't hesitate to call me if anything comes up. You have my direct number.

Assaf ordered another cup of coffee and stretched his long legs over the chair Boaz had vacated only a few moments earlier. '*Yes, I know what to do,*' he thought, fully aware of the sense of calm that was coming over him. '*The feeling of being at peace once you've come to a decision*'. In the course of any operation or tough decision, calm would eventually take over, replacing any doubts, any deliberations, ushering in resolve, tenacity and triumph.

The coffee was good. He enjoyed it fully, left the sweet waitress a nice tip, got into his Chevy Camaro and went home, back to his mansion.

*

- Security Inc., hello, how may I help you?

Seated on his plush CEO armchair in his luxurious study back at the mansion, Assaf replied:

- I would like to set up an appointment with Ido. Please tell him Assaf Shlomi is on the line, miss.

He knew Ido when the latter was head of security at Israel's General Security Service. After Ido retired, opting for early pension, he founded his own security company, which soon became renowned for its consummate expertise and high discretion.

- When can you come over? I require your assistance.
- How urgent is this for you?
- Very.
- Okay. Let me get rid of a few nags outside my door and I'll come over. What's the address?

Contrary to his image as chief of GSS security branch, Ido was small in stature and quite slim. He always had this pair of jeans that was a few sizes too big, a plaid shirt and old sandals, even in winter. From their very first meeting, back at *GSS* HQ in Jaffa, it occurred to Assaf this person had to be a real pro, seeing as nothing about his outward appearance spoke of either security or defense.

The same thought occurred to him an hour after Assaf called Ido's firm, when the latter entered Assaf's "modest digs". Nevertheless, Ido has a proven track record. He proved highly successful in establishing an excellent security department at GSS. His team withstood many tests and crises. All attempts to undermine the service's activities, in Israel and abroad, failed thanks to the clever and resourceful system that Ido had put in place. When Ido retired, he was highly sought after by numerous organizations and established firms that knew of him. They soon became his clients, along with new ones.

'*Here he is, small and full of admiration,*' Assaf relished the impression his mansion made on his guest.

- I've always maintained Mossad is a lot more generous than the GSS when it comes to its veterans' pensions.

- I'm not complaining, mind you, but rest assured my pension doesn't even cover my electric bill.

- You seem to be doing just fine. I heard you've done very well for yourself over the past ten years.

- True but, then again, you know what they say, "you can't take it with you"…

- So I'm guessing you called me over for the "take it *from* you" part?

- You guessed right. When I got the house insured, I added, per the insurance company's demands, all sorts of security measures, such multi-lock, alarm, sensors and so on. Nevertheless, in this day and age, one can't be too careful, and the manor's periphery need being up, security-wise. Security is your middle name, is it not?

- So what have you got in mind?

- I would like to have a security system around the house, complete with monitors and early detection so that I may have some peace of mind. I need to be sure no one can get in without being detected - without me knowing about it first.

- Are you concerned with anyone or anything in particular? We can set you up with what we call "an all-inclusive security package". You're not familiar with this term? It's a made-to-fit package, tailored to your exact needs, like a glove. I can offer you specific solutions to problem areas.

- No, that won't be necessary. I'd like you to give me a quote for a general extended collateral security package of the entire mansion. I'd like to emphasize one thing: we go back many years and all that, but I will pay same as anyone else. I might let you 'shave off' the order I once placed at that hummus place we used to go to.

- What are you talking about? You never asked me out. All we did was celebrate the successful bust on that gang from Romania. We were looking for some place to go to and have a feast, when someone suggested we simply cross the street and have at it. True, you did pick up the check for that, but I know for a fact the Mossad paid you back in full against the receipt you gave them. Just in case you doubt my words, I can show you the exact, itemized bill, so do not do me any favors. Spare me the 'shave off' talk.

- You're the best!

Assaf laughed and continued.

- What's next, Ido?

- I need the house blueprints by tomorrow, along with a detailed map of your land. My men will come over to pick it up and have a close look of the grounds for themselves. I'll be sending you my quote in a matter of days. Don't you worry about our bill, you'll get it, in full. You seem to have forgotten how it actually went down at that hummus place, but I never forgot it was *I* who picked up the tab at another place, where we had shakshuka. I've always hated keeping score and having to collect debts.

Security in and around the mansion was stepped up within days, complete with an electric gate and perimeter lighting, except for the stables, since "the horses need complete darkness during nighttime," as the people from Ido's company were told. In addition, they installed a hotline that connected the house directly to their operational command center.

Assaf would begin each day riding his horses, an old hobby of his, dating back to his childhood days on the moshav. When he had his dream house planned out, he had set a side ample room for stables, designing it with the best professional he could afford. He built his steeds three spacious stalls, an entire room where they could be washed and pampered, a training ring, a shed to store their feed, another room for their saddles and other riding accoutrements, and a tiny kitchenette just to have coffee there.

Assaf retained the services of Mohamed, a Bedouin groomer from the neighborhood, who was said to be a real horse whisperer. Mohamed would come to the stables each day, give each horse a bath, clean their hooves, brush their tail, check their teeth, clean their stalls, fix their saddles and feed them their hay each evening.

Assaf had three mares: two Arabian mares, one brown, the other black, whose pedigree were as long as they were graceful. The third, which he named Kochava (Star), was his pride and joy. He loved her more than anything. A purchase from a renowned and log-standing establishment in London, with whom Assaf had many dealings over many years.

One day, Assaf received a call from those horse traders: "Come quick. We have something special for you."

Two days later, he arrived at their old stables, situated at a farm outside London.

- The waiting list is long, but we've kept her just for you.

The mare took Assaf's breath away. *'This is the most beautiful horse I have ever seen,'* he immediately thought when they presented it before him.

Tall, long-tailed, full mane and bright gray with a star on its forehead, the mare immediately came over to Assaf the moment she laid her eyes on him. Stomping, waving her mane and neighing gleefully, the mare treated Assaf like her long lost twin brother. The dealer didn't need more than a second to smell a deal.

- This is a rare Quarter Horse Mare. I would like to show you her lineage and the clearance from the vet.

Assaf leafed through the paperwork just to go through the motions, for he knew he was about to acquire this mare, even if it were a mere cart-puller from the back of beyond.

- I'll give you a special price. A mere fifty thousand bucks.

Assaf and the horse trader arranged for the mare to be shipped to Israel within two months, after another course of training to complete its education.

Upon Kochava's arrival, Assaf saw she had a specially fitted handmade saddle, the handiwork of a world famous Saudi artisan, according to the note attached.

Years later, the seller confided in Assaf that he had regretted not selling him the mare for at least twice for the price, seeing as he would have paid whatever sum. Assaf would have indeed paid…

*

One day, Assaf was going over his international investments. When he happened to glance at the surveillance camera near his desk, he saw this black car parked up front. A few moments later, he looked again and saw that the car was still there. He took out his gun from the safe and came down to the gate. As soon as he stepped out of his house, Assaf spotted a familiar figure in the car. Nevertheless, he was amazed when saw it was indeed Eli at the wheel.

Still, he managed to steady his voice and control his facial features.

- What are you doing here?

- Just passing through. I happened to be in the neighborhood and they told me you've got a nice house. I stopped to have a look.

- Why didn't you tell me you were coming? Would you like to come in?

- I'm rather in a hurry. Besides, I don't know if have the time. Don't worry. I'll come calling. Sometime.

Eli was leaning over the steering wheel. Still tall and stern-faced, his hair turned white since the last time Assaf had seen him.

- So what would you like to do, Eli? No point standing by the side of the road.

- No. I'm off. Ah, before I forget, our mutual friend asked me to tell you he's still waiting for your answer.

Assaf wasn't at all surprised by that. He'd been waiting for this message the moment he recognized the man in the car.

- Tell your friend nothing happened and nothing will. He is sure to know what that means.

- I'll be sure to pass that along. By the way, I heard you've got some nice horses. I'd like to have a look sometime. Remember how much I love them?

Eli started the engine and drove off.

*

Assaf had thought he's seen it all, or practically everything and anything there was to see. He has been on dangerous assignments abroad, encountered his share of double agents, friends who were assassinated, various attempts on his own life and numerous other experiences he'd survived somehow, by the skin of his teeth. He wasn't at all scared. Far from it. He always believed in himself, and in the system he was operating within.

Nevertheless, he was feeling something new: being threatened. He didn't have the protection of the organization behind him, so without any cover, he had to entertain the option of caving in to Dudi's demands and pay up, but he rejected it outright. '*I am not the kind of man who succumbs to threats and blackmail. If you want war, you got it*,' he thought.

Assaf knew Boaz's secret number by heart. He began dialing his direct number but then let go of the dial. '*No, that's no solution. I am up against clever people who know how to play the system. I shall have to match their cruelty*,' he said to himself. As was his custom during moments of stress and deliberation, he took three sugar cubes and went down to the stables. He handed each of his two Arab horses a cube and let Kochava lick the third straight from the palm of his hand. She thanked him in her usual neighing. He looked at her wise eyes, rubbed her nose and returned home, calm and determined.

*

Every Friday, Assaf would go down to the village stores, pass through the local post office, do some shopping at the modest supermarket and have coffee at the local café with his usual friends there. One time he returned to his car, which he had parked at the local village parking lot, only to find a 9mm bullet under his windshield wiper.

- Hi Boaz, I hope I'm not interrupting you with anything.

- Did something happen?

- Someone left a bullet on the front shield of my car.

- Don't touch anything. Stay clear. Don't let anyone get close to your car. We're on our way.

Boaz appeared twenty minutes later, driving a car with civilian license plates. He looked worried and nervous.

- The forensics lab's car is on its way. But first, you have to hear the latest joke I heard on my way:

- This guy, you see, happened to come across a friend he hadn't seen in years. 'How are you? How's the family doing?' And the other answered, 'Everything's fine. You must have heard I got widowed three times already.' And so the guy says, 'Really? How sad. How did that happen?' so he replies, 'Well, my first wife died after eating poisonous mushrooms.' 'And your second wife?' 'She died after eating poisonous mushrooms too.' 'Oh. And the third?' 'She didn't wanna have any, so I had to strangle her myself.' Get it?

Assaf was never a man for jokes, but he humored his friend and gave a short laugh, just to be polite.

Two minutes later, the police car pulled up. The forensics team got out in their white overalls, sealed the perimeter around Assaf's car within the parking lot using their red security tape and began taking photographs from every direction. One of them put on a pair of white gloves, carefully removed the bullet from the windshield, placed it in an enveloped and made a record of the case. He then handed the envelope to another cop.

Two additional police officers were busy dusting the car's exterior in an attempt to find traces of fingerprints. Once they were done, the forensics team produced special equipment from their car, and used it to carefully examine the bottom of Assaf's car. Only once they were satisfied did they open the car's doors and check the interior. When they were finally done, they told Boaz they'll be in touch and went about their business.

- We need to talk.

- No problem. Follow me. Let's have coffee at your mansion.

Assaf poured each Boaz and himself a coffee on his spacious terrace, overlooking the fields. Boaz seemed troubled and pensive. After a brief silence, he looked at Assaf.

- I know you are familiar with Mossad code, but I know the codes the criminal world operate by. This is an escalation. That's what worries me. Someone has sent you a clear message. You'd better take it seriously.

- I'm doing just that. I stepped up security around the house. To tell you the truth, I never imagined anyone would dare place a bullet on my car in broad daylight and in such a public place.

- The people who are after you are clever and resourceful. What's more they are determined and unafraid. The business with the bullet today is small potatoes for them.

- How did they know that was my car? How did they know where I was?

That's exactly what I'm saying. That's bold and clever. Since you asked me in earnest, well, the answer is simple: you are being followed.

- So what do I do?

- I haven't been twiddling my thumbs all this time. Expecting this escalation, I instructed a few steps be taken concerning your friends from London. For your part, just be careful and watch every move you make. It's a good thing you beefed up security, but that's not enough. I've seen from experience how they manage to get around the toughest security measures. Here, I got you a special mirror to look under your car with. Use it every time you are about to enter your car. You have to check it from every angle, look around for anything that might be out of place. Never get in without looking under there! I'll be in touch.

He called Assaf the following day:

- Our inquiry revealed that Dudi went to Paris over three days ago and that Eli has been in Eilat for a week now. He stayed in his hotel room all day yesterday. We're continuing with our investigation.

Assaf was surprised to detect a sense of pride. '*I seem to have real adversaries,*' he mused, feeling quite self-important. '*After all, I did pick them for the operation in London 'cuz they're the best. But this time, they aren't with me. They are against me. Ah, well, I've been through tough situations before and survived all kinds of scrapes. I just need to stay focused and tenacious. That's how it went down back in Iran*', he recalled the Isfahan operation, when an Iranian agent he had previously turned and worked with for years suddenly put a gun to Assaf's head at that safehouse in Tehran and demanded the entire list of Mossad operatives in the country. It took courage, determination and creativity on Assaf's part, as well as those of the agents in the Mossad station in Tehran, to save his own life, along with "our fine boys". *'Yeah, it's gonna take all my ingenuity and grit to get outta this jam'.*

*

Dudi had a complex personality. When he hated, his animosity knew no bounds, and likewise, when he felt love, his ardor was enormous. He abhorred anyone who cheated him or betrayed his trust, and when he felt that someone had, he took revenge. Equally, he showed endless empathy and generosity to those he cared for.

His son Sephi was the one thing in this world he seemed to love the most. Those who got the taste of his ferocity, his dark side, would not have imagined he could be so tender, let alone picture him sitting on a small chair joining a sing-along of Hanukkah songs at his son's kindergarten. When he wasn't held up in interrogation rooms or detention cells, Dudi would show up for PTA meetings and involve himself as much as was humanly possible in his son's education.

Sephi was the exact opposite of the life Dudi was born into. Whatever Dudi was denied or could never receive or gain access to growing up, he would bestow on Sephi and shower him with it to no end. Sephi was his "closure". He couldn't be more proud when his son told him he wanted to volunteer to a combat unit. Ahead of his recruitment date, Dudi and Sephi trained as hard as possible. They would get up at the crack of dawn and run seven miles along the beach, after which Dudi would have his morning coffee at the beach café and Sephi would continue exercising not far away, making full use of the dunes and the fresh air.

And what would a proud and loving dad get his son on his joining the IDF? Sephi's parents took their son to the recruitment base and waited all day for him to complete the process. At the end of that day, Sephi was assigned to the paratroopers and was told to show up for basic training the following Sunday. When the three of them returned home from the base, Sephi was in for a surprise. There, by the coffee table in the living room, right next to the celebratory cake and flowers, he saw this fancy white envelope.

"Go ahead, open it," his parents urged him in excitement.

The envelope had a gorgeous set of keys. Dudi pulled his son to the balcony and pointed at the parking lot, where, right in the center, Sephi spotted a car the likes of which he had never seen for real, until then. He rushed out to get into his black Porsche convertible, complete with white tires and elaborate gadgetry. A dream come true. He could not resist taking it for a spin, a victory ride across Netanya, right before everyone's astonished looks. No one had ever seen such a car so close. When Sephi got back, he gave his parents a loving hug.

- How did you know? However did you guess that was my dream car? Trouble is, I don't want to go to the army now. How can I leave my car behind?

- This is our present to you, on the occasion of your joining the IDF. You'll go, you'll be the best you can be, you'll get your parachute wings, and, G-d willing, you'll go on to become an officer. Your Porsche and we will always be waiting for you here whenever you're on leave.

And so it was. Sephi began his long and arduous basic paratrooper training and graduated with flying colors, literally. Whenever he was back on his short leaves, he would hug his parents and go for a spin. He relished the jealous gazes of all his friends and the adoring eyes of all the girls. Before his basic training ended, he was awarded an entire week off and got home around midnight. He was so tired, he fell asleep right there and then, on his bed. The following day, he planned to take his girlfriend and another couple of friends up north in his car. Sephi woke up in the middle of the day and came down to polish his car. Much to his surprised, the Porsche wasn't there.

- Dad, come quick! The car's gone!

- Don't do anything. I'll be right there.

Dudi got home in ten minutes. He and Sephi patrolled the entire area, if only to refute the possibility the car had been parked elsewhere. No. It was gone alright.

- We have to go to the police.

- I will not inform the cops. I won't give'em that pleasure. I'll call the insurance agent.

The agent was taken aback when Dudi told him the car had disappeared. He could barely find an insurance company ready and willing to cover such an expensive and rare car. The premium Dudi paid was enough to buy your average family sedan.

The agent replied eventually:

- The insurance company will have my head for this, but it can't be helped. In any case, I need you to go to the police so that I can send the complaint forms to process your claim.

Luckily for Dudi, the Porsche was registered under Sephi's name. As far as Dudi was concerned, he didn't mind the insurance money. All he cared about was not going to the cops. He could already see it, '*I would have to face this junior duty officer who wouldn't be able to resist telling everyone that the great and powerful Dudi had to go to the police. They of course won't bother with the car's disappearance, all they'd care about was how I came up with the million bucks it cost in the first place.'* Nevertheless, Sephi went down to the station to lodge a complaint about the car getting stolen.

Dudi knew the real issue was that the car was supposed to be off limits. "The great and powerful" Dudi could not afford his son's car to get stolen. He could think of only one person who could have pulled this off. Two days passed and one of his men called him up: "Come quick to Smilanski Street."

There, by this tall building under construction, Dudi spotted a gathering crowd. As he drew closer, he saw they were looking up, so he followed their gaze, only to come across the most amazing scene: a shiny Porsche was dangling from a crane on the seventeenth floor!

A police car appeared from nowhere within two minutes, and out came these precinct officers. Dudi will never forget the gleeful screams and scornful looks they gave him, "the mighty Dudi", laughing at him for everyone to see. They gave him a hard time from the trick *someone* played on him all the way up the seventeenth floor.

*

One fine spring morning, as the first sunrays reached through the trees, brightening up the early hours of the day, waking the birds and ushering their changing of the guard with the night birds, Assaf woke to another one of his favorite times of the year. He took a quick shower before his morning ride, enjoying the rush of adrenaline matching the flow of cold water. He looked at himself in the mirror and happened to like what he saw: his firm body, flat stomach, thick hair and azure eyes. He has retained his vitality on top of his physique and looks. Satisfied with himself, he couldn't help thinking, *'they were wrong to think they could scare me or get the better of me,'* to which he added a hint of a smirk as he dried himself off: *'they seemed to have forgotten I was a whiz, how ingenious I can be. Yes, I could have swung that car up the thirtieth floor, but that would have been too showy. I hope that would serve as enough of a hint they shouldn't mess with me and stop trying to shake me down'.*

Having wiped himself completely dry, he went to his dressing room and put on the riding breeches he had purchased on his last trip to London. He then put on his riding boots and an Israeli brand plaid riding shirt. Last, he put on a blue riding cap, his constant companion that he'd bought at the flea market in Jaffa. *'I'll have coffee later, at the stables,'* he said as he picked up the usual sugar cubes and went out to the porch. *'Hmm, it's usually not that peaceful by this time,'* he observed, slightly surprised.

Kochava would greet Assaf each morning with her usual elated sounds, as though she'd been up since dawn, expecting the daily pampering and morning ride in the dew-filled fields. *'It's too quiet'.* The silence was beginning to bother him to the point of anxiety with each step towards the stalls. The two Arabian horses, who would look on, envious of him and Kochava, looked away this time. He didn't see her anywhere. *'She must be waiting further inside,'* he quickened his pace, but as he got there, his entire world came crashing down, for there she was, laying on her side, her mane over her eyes, her legs still swinging in midair.

Assaf collapsed immediately. He couldn't help himself. He

cried. He, who had never shed a tear, not even when they told him his mother, to whom he felt closest in particular, had died. This time, the tears just kept on pouring. He never felt so lost, so desperate. A few moments later, he recovered slightly, well, enough to drag himself over to the phone.

The vet arrived very quickly.

- There's nothing I can do. Kochava was poisoned. I found the toxin between its teeth. Mohamed will dispose of the body once the police are gone.

Not too long after that, Boaz got out of his police car.

- I'm here. The forensics lab team is on its way. They'll look for leads at the scene.

Assaf's fatigue and misery were all that prevented him from blurting out his exact opinion about the chances of finding any clues. He didn't need any evidence as to whodunnit, he already knew.

- There's another reason I'm here. The local chief of police wants to see you.

- I have no intention of availing myself. The last thing I wanna see right now is another police officer.

- I figured you might say that, Assaf. Look, I have warrant for your arrest. If you're unwilling to come on your own accord, it's going to get very embarrassing.

Assaf was too depressed and worn out to resist, so he went along with Boaz down to the district police station, where, the local police commander saw him. "Don't get me wrong, Assaf. You're not a suspect. I merely got a protective custody warrant for you.

- I don't get it.

- Oh, I think you do. Your life's in danger. You may do what you will, but I will not risk my career by letting you get yourself killed on my watch.

- So what are you proposing?

- Leave the country, at least until things die down, or at least until we can guarantee your safety.

- You mistake me for someone who runs from a fight. I never turn away from danger. I always face it head on, and I am not about to start running away now. I can take care of myself.

- That's exactly what I'm worried about.

Only after a few rounds of this argument, did they agree that Assaf would be allowed to return home, where a police car would be assigned on a regular basis, on top of a team of private security guards at the mansion.

*

The meeting was arranged for ten am at one of Tel Aviv's luxury towers. He was hoping that finally, after so much negotiation, the Indian firm's rep would be so kind as to conclude the consultancy agreement Assaf had worked so hard to hammer out. He had some laundry to drop off at the village on the way, so he turned left at the square to park in the public parking lot, when some other car suddenly rammed the back of his own car very forcefully. When Assaf got out of his car to survey the damage, he heard the beginning of the nine o'clock news on the car radio, and before he knew it, a great big bang tore through everything. Assaf was blown way up in the air, only to land on a patch of grass, in one piece, a few feet away of what used to be his car. Half of it was gone. That's all he could make out when he lifted his head, a few seconds later. The image barely sunk in. Much to his surprise, the front half of his car had vanished. Even more surprisingly, the back seat and the back half remained intact. Another car, driven by this woman, who was now in shock, was lodged into the remains of Assaf's car.

The people at the nearby village coffee shop rescued her and gave her some cold water.

Assaf graciously said he was okay when they came to his side. Even then, he was still in command of his senses.

- I'm fine. Thanks. See to her.

The all too familiar forensics team's car soon appeared at the scene. "That's the work of a pro, right there," their commander told Boaz as soon as he arrived, which was right away. Boaz brought over additional investigators in his car.

Boaz could hardly speak. He didn't have a joke to tell this time. He just kept looking in disbelief. Assaf remained stoic. He didn't need forensics to tell him what's what. Later that day, when Boaz called, Assaf remained calm when he heard that "Dudi had left Israel two days ago. Eli has been on vacation up north for three days now, cherry picking with his family."

CHAPTER 27

It was July 13 at ten pm when the intercom buzzed at Eli's apartment on Tel Aviv's busy King George Street. An unknown man asked him to come down and sign for a personal envelope, but there was no one there when he reached the front door of his building. Eli was about to turn around and go back up, when some guy in black emerged from the dark, fired three shots at Eli's back and escaped on a motorcycle. Eli's wife heard the shots and came down, only to find her husband flat on the floor, unconscious. The ambulance that quickly arrived took Eli to the nearby Ichilov Hospital, where they saved his life, only to be released many months later, still paralyzed from the neck down.

The police investigation revealed nothing. The expert opinion of physicians and officers from the major crimes department was that Eli sustained two 9mm shots. Eli did not agree. He also rejected the pathology report that showed two entry and exit wounds. Nothing could make him change his mind, which remained as intransigent as his body was stiff. He could only move his lips.

- He shot me three times.

- But how do you know?

You guys may have found two shots, but I *know* there were three.

Eli knew the age old service maxim: "Always fire three times. The third is to verify the kill."

He spent the following years in a wheelchair, paralyzed from his neck down, tended to by two Filipino male nurses. All this time, he did nothing but think. He had no idea who pulled the trigger, but he knew for sure who it was who sent him. Being the only person who could settle the score, he constantly prayed to return to his feet and get his revenge. Nevertheless, the injuries he had sustained made the chances of any real recovery slim. One day, a caretaker found him dead in his bed.

CHAPTER 28

That was *their* beach. They were always alone between the gravel hills and the pebbly beach, running off from school and sharing their secrets. They knew almost every grain of sand, the curves and shapes of the seaweed covered rocks, the small pools and ponds, and even the tiny crustaceans that lurked there, hunting and being hunted.

The rocks and pebbles kept most people at bay, as that part of the beach did not make for a pleasant stroll on soft white sands. That suited Assaf and Dudi perfectly.

Once, Dudi and Assaf discovered an underwater tunnel inside the bedrock and realized they could swim through it all the way to the open sea. They quickly made this their routine, with nothing but the sea to keep them company. They loved the beating waves and stormy, 'oceanic' surroundings, which they found beautiful as well as challenging. When the Mediterranean was more placid, they relished the sun and the calm waves, diving and floating like dolphins or seals.

When they would get tired, they'd lie on the soft sand and let the peace and quiet engulf them. When evening was about to descend, they would head back to the hills and marvel at the setting sun, by the bushes that bloomed at dusk in full yellow blossoms.

Those many days of spending so much time together brought Dudi and Assaf very close. So much so, that even after they had drifted apart, they still came to their private refuge, each in his own time.

*

Dudi had just concluded a meeting with his operations guy. '*Time for some alone time*'. He told his driver to take him to the beach. A little before arriving, he instructed him to stop the luxurious BMW and made the rest of the way on foot. He saw his other car, with his own security detail, overtaking his car, parking on the edge of the cliff. Two of his bodyguards came down and surveyed the empty beach, keeping their distance.

He took off his white shirt, folded it carefully and laid it on a nearby rock, where he then placed his tailored pants along with his Calvin Klein briefs, from his favorite store in Paris. He lay flat on his back, immersed in the sun's caresses over his naked body. He got into the water about half an hour later and swam towards the secret passage to the underwater tunnel. He took a long breath and dived to the other side. When he emerged on the side of the open sea, he floated on his back and took in the peace and quiet. The sun and the waves warmed his chest and lullabied him. The water felt so good on his back.

About a yard away, a scuba diver in black emerged. He had on large goggles. He attached his hand gun to Dudi's skull and fired. The waves and the wind drowned out the sound of the three shots. The figure dove back into the sea.

It took some time until Dudi's bodyguards became concerned, seeing as he would usually return after a while. They scanned the entire beach for their boss, but only after a few long minutes did they spot his naked body. He was flat on his back, nestled, dangling in the waves.

CHAPTER 29

A line of beautiful Polynesian girls greeted the Air France flight when it landed in Papeete, Tahiti's capital, offering the tourists rum and sliced pineapple. The passengers, in turn, could not help but marvel at their straw skirts and the lotus flowers in their hair.

Passing through customs and passport control was as congenial and pleasant as the girls were. Sali Solon produced his French passport and his light hand luggage. Since that was all he had to declare, he was out of the terminal in no time. He took an adorned cab all the way to the marina across town. He waited but a short while before boarding a ferry to Mo'orea, the most enchanted of all Tahitian islands. From the moment he set foot on deck, it felt like a dream come true, as this was indeed a lifelong dream of his.

He soon found himself at the lavish bungalow overlooking Cooks Bay, which he had reserved so long before. He let out this long, liberating laughter. '*This must be the way Adam felt,*' he told himself.

The bay was surrounded by this lagoon, whose waters were so clear, he could see all the way to the bottom, complete with a myriad of fish in every conceivable color. '*The sand is even whiter and softer than in Netanya,*' he mused. The palm trees strewn across the beach nearly reached the very waterline. '*It's like they're kissing the waves*'.

Two local girls were waiting for him by his cabin, their brown skin glistening in the sun. His azure eyes made them laugh. They invited him to sit with them on the decorative beach beds and take in the boundless beauty as they handed him a cup of fizzy mango wine.

'*Who said it's a hard life?*' he thought, helping himself to the girl on his right as the girl on the left raised the cup to his lips. '*I only wish I knew how he came to know about the Isfahan affair*'.

Made in the USA
Middletown, DE
05 August 2020